The Daughters of Time, Book 1

The Secrets of the Clock

C.S. Kjar

Editor: JoEllen Claypool
Cover Designed by jimmygibbs
Proofreading by John Buchanan and Julie Gunter

Available in eBook and Paperback

Paperback ISBN: 978-0-9985897-2-5
Digital ISBN: 978-0-9985897-3-2

http://cskjar.com

This book is the result of a workshop given by the Idaho Creative Authors Network (ICAN) in Boise, Idaho. During one of the workshop exercises, my tablemates and I quickly plotted an outline of this tale. I was so excited about it I told them I would write this book. I'm proud to dedicate this book to Lance and Pamela Thompson and Arimenta Self, and to the ladies of ICAN. Thanks so much for your inspiration and support!

Chapter 1

Francis and Father Time

The waning days of summer baked the white stone cottage by the Florida beach. Inside, the waning days of Francis Elizabeth Time stretched thin over her cancer-wracked body in the little bed. She faded in and out, sometimes sleeping, sometimes listening to the rustling of her husband in the room and the occasional visit from the hospice nurse.

Outside, the lapping of the ocean's waves against the shore comforted Francis. She would have been in total peace except for the incessant beeping from the monitor beside her bed. Like a clock ticking off to the final countdown, the monitor beeped off the counts to her final heartbeat.

And it was driving her crazy!

The beeping picked up speed, triggering the hospice nurse to run in from the other room. She checked Francis, then the lines running from Francis to the machine. Pressing buttons and checking tubes, she could find nothing wrong.

"Silence that monitor before it drives me crazy!" Francis bellowed from her deathbed. "It's bad enough to be dying, but to listen to that maddening noise while I do it is too much!"

The nurse quickly muted the beeping and watched the monitor's line bob more slowly as the patient calmed down. "There now, Miss Francis," she said a voice as starched as her uniform, "I've put the monitor on mute. Try to stay calm."

Too weak to argue, but too determined to not die yet, Francis dismissed the nurse and called for her husband. "Where are you, honey?"

Father Time, bent over her. "I'm here, sweetheart," he whispered, stroking her cheek. "What can I do for you?"

Opening her eyes, Francis saw his face not far above hers. This time of year, her husband looked sixty years old, with gray hair around his temples and dignified crow's feet beside them. She loved him at all his ages during the year, but especially at this one.

"Let's talk," she whispered in a lover's tone.

Father Time raised the head of her hospital bed a bit, then sat in the chair beside her where he'd kept many days' vigil. "You've never ceased to amaze me, Franny dear. Here you are on the verge of entering the next world, and you still want to talk."

"No time for compliments, dear. I must make sure I've done everything I can for our daughters. Time is short, and there's so much to do. Help me run through the list again."

Releasing a sigh of someone doing something for the umpteenth time, Father Time began the well-rehearsed list, holding up his fingers as he counted the items off. "You've transferred the title of the house to our girls. You wrote a letter that your lawyer will give to them, telling them what to do. You made the video that tells them about the clock. You hid the video so they will not be able to find it easily. Your will is with that shyster lawyer..." He dropped his hand and shook his head. "Franny, I disagree with how you're going about this. Let me call the girls and tell them to come see you one last time."

She'd thought it out carefully. There was no time left to change anything. "No!" Francis struggled to raise herself from the bed. "It will work..."

Father Time quickly stood and pushed her gently back. "Okay, Franny, I'll do it your way."

She was too weak to put up a struggle. She let him settle her back and straighten the light cover over her again.

He adjusted her oxygen tubes, then sat beside her again. He ran a thin hand through his hair, pausing it on the back of his neck. His shoulders slumped as he slouched into the chair.

The effort to rise tired Francis more than she thought it would. Closing her eyes, she drifted off to sleep.

When she awoke again, the sky was filled with stars. The sound of the ocean waves caressing the beach was a soothing whisper to her ears. She'd always loved the sound of the waves as they came toward her cottage.

Father Time stood at the window, looking out at the moon's long reflection on the water.

"My love," she whispered. As soon as the words

left her lips, he moved to her side. "Where were we on my list?"

In the dim glow from the heart monitor, she saw a small smile spread across his worry-creased face. He stroked her cheek, and the line of her heart monitor bounced faster.

Father Time aged a little more every day. Francis loved the excitement of being with the man who aged rapidly, but like the mythical phoenix, became young again each new year. They could only be seen in public when their ages matched each other, but that didn't mean he didn't spend time with her in this magical cottage. They'd spent many many years together thanks to the clock.

Father Time planted a soft kiss on her forehead. "You've done everything, even though I don't agree with your methods. Leaving it to our girls to settle their differences on their own is risky. And bringing in that crazy lawyer of yours is like adding dynamite to the flame."

Francis moved her head on the pillow, signaling her disagreement. "It's the only way we can make our daughters become family again. Hannah will never forgive her sisters for ruining her wedding. Essie's too proud to make the first move, and Sharon's too scared to get anywhere near conflict."

Weakness overtook Francis as she fought off the urge to fall asleep, maybe for good this time. She moved her leg slightly to get her heart to beat more. She paused before drawing a deep breath.

"No, this is the best way. Giving them a common enemy will give them something to face together. They'll have to unite to save the cottage. Then peace will return to the family."

Father Time got up from the edge of her bed and went back to the window. "I find it hard to forgive them for not coming to see you more. They turned their back on each other and on you, their mother! You had nothing to do with that row at the wedding. Goodness knows we tried to get everyone to calm down, but it was no use." He turned to face her. "I'm disappointed in them."

"Don't be. They're not bad girls. I've watched them in the clock. They're happy with their lives now. It's what we wanted for them. They spread joy and love around the world. What more could we have asked from them?"

Fatigue took over Francis, but she pushed it aside. Not much time was left, and there were things still to say. "But they're so far apart. In heart because of past grudges, and in miles because they live all over the globe. That's your doing, you know. You're the one who introduced them to their husbands."

Father Time chuckled and stroked his graying beard. "You encouraged them. There's more than enough blame to go around. They married a good assortment of men, even as odd as some of them may be. Easter Bunny is a good ol' guy and Santa Claus is the best. I had reservations about Hannah with Headless Horseman, but he's good to her, which makes me like him. He may look scary, but he has a good heart."

Francis nodded and smiled. "Mortals with immortals. A lovely life, but it will come to an end someday. Their husbands will go on and find others."

"But their children will carry the tale of their

special lives. Do you regret marrying an immortal?"

A smile spread across the dying woman's face. She regretted nothing where her husband was concerned. They'd had a good life together. Only one regret remained. Her fractured family.

Father Time moved back to the chair and took his wife's hand. "I still think our daughters should be here now. Maybe even their families with them. Let me call them. We could bring them together before you..." His voice choked.

"No. Promise me you'll do it my way."

Father Time wiped his eyes, then whispered, "I promise."

"It's more peaceful this way. No crying or regrets or old resentments around me. Just you and me and the sea."

The sound of the ocean played a mournful song for the couple facing the end of their time together on earth. Still, Francis couldn't be too sad. The ocean would remain, and the tides would still come and go. The stars and the moon would look the same for her daughters and grandchildren. Life would go on. Time would go on.

Her husband stood and leaned over her again, kissing her lips softly. He held her face gently in his hands, he whispered, "I searched for a millennium to find a woman like you to love. It will be at least that long or longer until the world is graced with another one like you." He kissed her again. "I will love you forever."

Peace enveloped her, pushing out any remaining fear or apprehension. "And I'll always love you. Because of you, I've lived an amazing life." She pulled her hand up with what little strength she had and covered his.

Sleep was clawing at her, threatening to pull her away from her lover. She moved her other leg a little to rouse herself. Words still needed to be said. Too little time was left to sleep it away.

Father Time stroked her hair beside her face. "What do you want me to do if our daughters don't come?"

"If they don't come, take the clock back with you. If they don't want the cottage, destroy it. Ask your friend Mother Nature to knock it down. Won't you, please?"

"If you wish it, I will do it."

Thankful for the darkness, Francis felt tears roll down the side of her face. A sniff came involuntarily.

Father Time got a tissue and wiped away her tears, her sniffles, and her last concern.

All was settled. Her life's work was done.

For a long while, the sound of the ocean filled the silence between them. Francis knew the girls would come. She willed them to come with all that was left in her. She had no doubt in her heart. She'd spent months preparing for everything. Her plan to restore her family would work. It would work. It would work.

A gray sky welcomed Father Time to the new day. As the moon went down, he'd watched as the heart monitor line went flat. A last weak breath and his bride of many years was gone. He said his final goodbye before waking the nurse to start the notifications as required, except for their daughters.

According to her wishes, he'd have her cremated and scatter her ashes in the ocean. After that, there was nothing to do until later. He would go back to work in the universe. As much as he didn't like it, he wouldn't deviate from her plan. He'd made a promise.

Chapter 2

Essie

Essie Bunny leaned against the kitchen cabinet in her underground house in Germany. Sylvie, one of her 13-year-old daughters, whined, cried, and stomped while she scrubbed on a blackened casserole dish in the sink.

The girl's soprano voice almost shattered the glass. "It wasn't my fault! Pete distracted me with his video game. He should be punished too!"

Essie waved away the protest. "You know the rules, young lady. You make a mess, you clean it up." She pointed at the sink. "Get your elbow grease out and scrub."

Sylvie wailed like her life was over as she carried out her sentence. "It's so unfair!"

With a roll of her eyes, Essie turned away from the ranting. As the mother of thirteen noisy, whiny, runny-nosed, bickering, unappreciative, smarter-than-my-parents kids, she'd heard it all. Sylvie knew the rules, and Essie's role as mother was to make her daughter abide by them.

"Sweetheart!" Essie's husband, Easter, poked his

head in the kitchen. The tall, lean man with big ears and buck teeth sorted through a handful of envelopes. "There you are! You have a letter!" He waved an envelope at Essie.

"Did I get anything, Pops?" A pretty teenage girl, stuck her head around her dad, looking at him with the pleading eyes of someone who wants to feel important.

Easter shook his head. "No love letters today, Marcia. Sorry!" Ignoring her moan of disappointment, he looked at his wife again. "Did you hear me? You have a letter from some law firm."

Sylvie ran in front of her father with tear-filled eyes, pleaded with him to get her out of scrubbing the black pan.

Easter took one look in the sink and laughed. "No wonder we had sandwiches for supper last night. Do what your mother told you to do."

Essie snapped her fingers and pointed at the sink. The dejected girl returned to her scrubbing.

After wiping her hands with a kitchen towel, Essie threw it on her shoulder. "A letter from who?" Walking closer to her husband, she pulled the letter from his hand and looked at it. The address read Essie Bunny, 410 Underhill Road, Germany. That was her, all right.

The return address was in the United States. Florida.

Essie's heart froze, then beat again. The only person she knew living in Florida was her mother. Why would a lawyer write to her?

"I hope nothing's happened to Mother." She turned the envelope over in her hands, afraid to open it. The news inside the envelope might break her heart. Or change her life. Or many other dreadful things.

Three small children gathered around her, pulling on her stained apron. "Mom, can we have a cookie? We're hungry!"

Seeing the envelope in her hands, one of her sons made a grab for it, but she pulled it out of his reach. She gave a mother's frown at the offender, who quickly backed away from her and put his brothers between her and him.

Easter gathered the trio and guided them out of the kitchen. "Kids, why don't you run along and find something useful to do before I find something for you. Your mother and I need time to talk. You too, Sylvie. The pan can soak for a few minutes."

Sylvie let out a whoop and ran from the kitchen so fast the kitchen curtains swayed slightly in her wake. Children scattered every direction, including those who'd been listening from the hallway.

Easter and Essie stood alone in the kitchen. "When was the last time you saw your mother?"

"At Hannah's wedding," Essie replied as the memory forced a shudder from her. "That awful wedding. Her color was black, like a funeral. The odd collection of his friends—or freaks as I call them. Ghosts and creatures of every ilk. The color reflected how the whole affair turned out." She rubbed her temples as the memory triggered a recurring headache.

Easter nodded as he raised his eyebrows. "I have to admit it. There were people there that made even me look normal. Very strange affair. But I don't think what you did helped the situation."

Essie frowned and glared at her husband His

remark opened her Pandora's box of bad memories tucked away in the dark recesses of her mind.

Memories of her mother, fashionably dressed as mother of the bride. Her rotund sister Sharon in her customary red dress. The bride, her younger sister Hannah, dressed in widow's weeds. Black and ugly. But why not. She married a man whose head was not attached to his body.

Visions of hateful words spoken too loudly in the wrong places and to the wrong people swirled like a cyclone in her head. Unforgiveable words had broken her family apart forever.

Rubbing her forehead, trying to push the memories back into the box, she went down the hallway to her bedroom. The black wedding day marked the end of her family as she'd known it. She never heard from her sisters. The occasional calls to and from her mother were all she had after that.

Her mother had liked her sisters more than her. Or at least it seemed like it. Despite that, she bore no ill will toward her mother. She'd made a good life for herself here in Germany with her family. She didn't care about either of her sisters. She didn't need them in her life any more.

Easter came up behind her and turned her to face him. "I'm here for you."

Essie looked at her husband's tender face and loving eyes. He had been born without cartilage in his nose so it hung down, making his nostrils seem like slits. She didn't mind what he looked like outwardly because she saw what was on the inside. Easter Bunny was a good man who worked hard to make sure children everywhere had fun finding treats one spring day each year.

Essie put the letter in her apron pocket. "I'm not going to read this now. I have too much to do."

She returned to the kitchen with Easter hot on her heels. She reached down into the sink and started scrubbing on the black pot. It wasn't charcoal she was scrubbing away, but her anxiety and grief over what became of the family she'd once been a part of.

Easter pulled on her arm. "Why wait? The news in that letter won't change. And who knows, it might be good news. Let's face it now. Together." He took the towel off her shoulder and dried her hands. Pulling her to the kitchen table, they sat together.

Getting the letter out of her pocket, she looked at the names on the envelope. Howard, Cannet, Bee, and Goforet, Attorneys at Law. Her hands trembled slightly as she tore the envelope open. The stationery she pulled out was crisp and had an expensive feel to it. She gently unfolded the letter to reveal its news.

Dear Mrs. Bunny:
We regret to inform you that your mother, Francis Time, passed away of cancer on the 9th day of August.

Essie grabbed her chest to keep her heart from falling out. Her mother was dead. A cry of anguish escaped her lips as the letter slipped out of her hand.

Easter leaned down and picked up the letter from where it had fallen on the floor. He read the letter, mumbling the words as she muffled her sobs.

Essie managed to choke out the words. "The ninth of August? That was two months ago. Why didn't someone call?"

She grabbed the letter from Easter, but her vision

was too blurred by tears to read it. She shoved it back at him. "What else does it say?"

He mumbled as he scanned the letter. "Your father took care of the funeral arrangements..."

"My father? My never-at-home father?" Essie stood up and paced, releasing some of the anger building inside. "Without contacting me? Oh sure, he's an important man in the universe and all, but the least he could have done was called!"

Easter kept reading the letter. "It also says there's a ticket for you to fly to Sarasota, leaving next week. Go see your dad and ask him about it." He rose to pull his wife back to her seat so he could rub her back, massaging in the right places to ease her tension.

His fingers felt good, but did little to ease her worry. "Did you say next week? Isn't that when the shipments of chocolate come in?"

Essie didn't hear his answer as her body jerked with the lightning bolt of fear shooting through her. Her sisters might be there. Her sisters who hated her.

Essie picked up the letter to look at it again. "Do you think Sharon and Hannah got the same letter?" On the second page, she saw it. "There's the cc list. They did."

A tear rolled down her cheek, and Easter wiped it away. He put his head against the side of hers and whispered in her ear, "What are you feeling?"

"Sad, mad, and confused," she whispered back. "Mom had cancer and never called to tell me. She's gone, and it seems I must face my sisters without her, and who knows how that will turn out."

She gulped hard to stifle the oncoming sob. "We hated each other when we left the wedding. I don't think feelings have changed."

Easter pushed a stray tress behind her ear. "You have to go find out. Maybe time has softened your sisters. Maybe you can find peace with them. Maybe your mother left money to you."

Her brain tripped over the suggestion. "This is not about money! It's — "

Two of their sons came in the kitchen, chattering away. They poured themselves glasses of milk, ignoring their parents who sat quiet and still at the table. Their chattering never stopped as they raided the cookie jar and left.

Essie folded the lawyer's letter and put it back in the envelope. She gave it to Easter.

Her heart ached, but she didn't dare let anyone other than Easter know it. If she got upset, her thirteen children would get upset, and chaos would ensue. Calm was too hard to restore with fifteen people, three dogs, two cats, and forty-three rabbits. Like her mother, she hated a big hubbub about anything. It was best to cry in private.

Needing to be alone, Essie pushed Easter away and went quickly to her bedroom, shutting the door on everyone and their needs.

Her mother was gone, leaving an empty hole no one else would ever fill. Grief welled up and spilled over in a flash flood of tears that ended almost as abruptly as it had started. Fourteen people depended on her. Life went on.

Seeing a stray sock on the floor, she picked it up and took it to the hamper in the bathroom. Her reflection in the mirror caused her to stop and stare back at the face that looked much like her mother's. At least how her mother had looked the last time she'd seen her at Hannah's wedding, almost fifteen years ago. There, her mother had had red, puffy eyes, like hers. Tears clouded the image as she turned to go back into her bedroom.

Kneeling on the floor, she pulled a large shoebox out from under the bed and opened it. Photographs were piled on each other in disarray. She dried her face with her t-shirt before reaching in. Sorting through the jumbled photos, she resolved to organize them someday.

Thumbing through a handful, she found the photo she prized most, with her mother and sisters standing in front of a small, whitewashed stone house with the peaked roof and large front porch. The young Essie stood there, tall and proper, her clothes neat and tidy, and her long hair drawn back in a ponytail. Her sister Sharon with her short wavy hair wore an apron over her dress, with her arms around their mother's waist. Her sister Hannah sat on the porch railing with two skinned knees, sandy bare feet, and a dark braided pigtail on each shoulder. The broad smiles on their faces reflected the happy times together at the cottage on the beach. Back in the days when they got along.

She shuffled through a few more photos until she found the other one she was looking for. A young girl with a freckled face and a missing front tooth smiled at her, and Essie couldn't help but smile back. The child that was her looked like some of her daughters. Where had the years gone?

"Mom?" A small voice came through the door. "What are you doing?" Small fingernails scratched on the door, making Essie's skin crawl.

Essie clenched her jaw and wondered what she had to do to get a moment of quiet. She quickly dumped the photos into the box and slid it back under the bed. Not wanting to answer the summons, she sat quietly, hoping the child would go away.

The scratching at the door continued until she couldn't stand it any longer. Going to the door, she opened it a crack and said, "What do you want?"

Her daughter Sue's five-year-old eyes looked up at her and tried to look behind her into the room. The question "what are you doing?" was etched on her face as she tried to look around her mother for answers.

Right behind her was Jenny, her triplet sister, with the same expression who asked, "Why is your door closed?"

Essie heaved a sigh and leaned against the door frame. No rest for a weary mother.

"I'll be out in a little bit. Go tell Jason to get you cookies from the jar. He's already been in there this afternoon." She watched as the girls smiled and skipped off down the hallway holding hands.

She started to close the door, but something stopped it. A firm push made her step back. Her husband's head came around the door.

"How are you doing?" He stepped inside and pulled her to him. Easter massaged her back again and held her tight.

Essie stepped away from him and took the letter from his pocket. "I know I'm supposed to go see this lawyer, but I'm not sure you can handle the kids and the factory. I should send my regrets."

Easter frowned. "No, you should go. Go settle matters with your mother. The kids and I will do fine without you — I mean, we can get along without you — I mean, we need you — we'll miss you and all — "

Essie laughed and put her finger over his lips to stop him from continuing his foot-in-mouth blathering. "Okay, I'll go," she whispered in case there were listening ears at the door. "I wonder what she'll do with her house. It's not much. Just an old stone house at the beach with a few acres of sand and grass around it. She only had old furniture and a grandfather clock that never worked. Shouldn't take long to dispose of it all." In her mind's eye, she could see every detail of her childhood home.

Easter smiled at her. "Our kids would love to see the place where you grew up. We could save our pennies and visit someday. Or if you decide to sell it and split the money with your sisters, we could use your part for a vacation next summer. We haven't had a big vacation anywhere since the kids were born."

Essie put the kibosh on that notion with a shake of her head. "A trip would be nice, but what we need more is an upgraded kitchen. The girls and I cook so much that we could use more room and better appliances."

Easter turned to leave. "We'll decide later, after we know if she left anything and how much." He gave her a wink and left.

Excitement, grief, and dread swirled inside Essie like a cyclone, uprooting even more emotions and tossing them around. Her mother was gone, but she might have a little extra money to help around the house. Her sisters would be in Florida, but it would absolutely be the last time she'd have to see them.

The next morning, the dining room of Easter and Essie was full of people, noise, dirty dishes, and motion as they finished breakfast around the long table. Boys tugged on girls' hair and ran back to their seats. Girls yowled and called for justice to be done. Kids screaming. Crying. Yelling. Calling for Mom. Bedlam.

The racket of thirteen children and three barking dogs was almost too much for Essie. She yelled to make herself heard above the din, but her efforts fell on unhearing ears.

She rubbed her temples to fight back the headache stress was causing. Time was short and the list of instructions was long. How could she get it all in before she left? She had to tell them about the meals in the freezer, how to run the washer, the dentist appointments for the triplets, picking up after the dogs...

With no warning, the light over the dining table went out and quiet was instantaneous. In a calm manner, Easter said, "Children, sit down and shut your mouths. Family meeting."

The sound of chair legs and benches being scooted around on the tile floor echoed through the room. Thirteen bodies sat around the long wooden table quietly, their eyes fixed on their parents.

Essie joined her husband at the head of the table as Easter brought the meeting to order. "As you know, Mother is leaving to go to Florida to settle the affairs of your grandmother."

A hand waved in the air. Without waiting to be recognized, Clara said, "Why can't we go with her?" She quickly put her hands back in her lap as a chorus of "yeah!" filled the room.

Easter paused with an amused look on his face. "Because we can't afford to buy plane tickets for everyone. Anyone want to volunteer to stay behind?" He looked around. "Since no one wants to stay behind, we'll wait until we can all go."

Essie looked at her children in the hand-me-down clothes and felt a small pang of guilt. "I wish I could take you with me, but as your father said, I can't. But, when I get back, we'll make a plan on how we can go visit Florida."

Smiles returned to the young faces, and the noise level started to grow.

Waving his arms to lower the din before it got out of hand again, Easter said in a loudspeaker voice, "I'm sorry you've never met your grandmother in America. I only met her twice, but I can tell you she was a kind woman who loved your mother and would've loved all of you too. Right, dear?"

Essie smiled as she noticed her mother's features in her daughters. No doubt about that. She had been a loving mother. From her example, Essie had learned how to be a good mother.

Her eyes burned. She looked down at her hands, ordering herself to regain control. "Yes, she'd have loved you. It makes me sad thinking about how you never met her. She was there for me, like I try to be with you."

Easter touched her arm and took over. "We have to pitch in to make sure everything gets done while Mom's gone. We have a schedule written on the wall calendar. Check it every day to see where you need to go and what you're expected to do. Plus, you older children, you'll be responsible for watching out for the younger ones while I'm working in the factory. Keep them out of trouble. Girls will wash dishes one night, and the boys will wash them the next night, and so on. I'll take volunteers on who wants to cook. Cooks don't have to wash dishes."

Hands shot up in the air and Easter negotiated a schedule that was satisfactory with all. The family decided Pete and Marcia would take care of the laundry since they were the oldest and Marcia knew how to run the washer. The next oldest, Sylvie and Clara, would make breakfast for everyone. Cereal, toast, and milk would be on the menu until Mother got back, with pancakes made by Easter served occasionally as a special treat.

Sadie, Thomas, Jason, and Stacy would hoe and pick the garden and do the yardwork. The youngest children, Alan, Sarah, Sue, Jenny, and Ned would pick everything up before going to bed, with the help of the older children. Everyone would make sure the house was tidy and neat for the next day.

With the chores assigned, the meeting was adjourned.

Before the chaos could begin again, Essie stood and asked everyone to stay seated. She cleared her throat of the lump forming before she spoke. "Thank you for pitching in to help your dad while I'm gone." She swallowed hard, trying to dislodge the lump reforming in her throat. "I'll be home soon, and I hope you'll take care of each other until then. I love you all."

Sarah meekly slid off the bench and came to hug her mother's waist. That started a chain reaction, and the children swarmed Essie. She hugged and kissed each child and sent them on to the van. She choked back a sob as the last one vanished around the corner.

Easter quickly came to her and gave her a giant hug that squeezed the heartache back inside.

Her heart ached, and she hadn't left yet. "I've never been away from my babies," she said, choking on her tears. "I should stay." An unpleasant thought arose and jolted her. "What if they find out they can take care of themselves and don't need me anymore?"

Easter laughed softly. "Your children will always need you. And if they learn how to take care of themselves, we've done our job. We don't want lazy moochers on our hands, do we?"

He laughed again when a slight smile made its way onto Essie's face. He took her in his arms and gave her a warm hug and a peck on the cheek. "Stop worrying! We have your back. You'll be home before you know it and maybe we'll have money to remodel the kitchen. Wouldn't that be fun!"

Essie looked in the old kitchen. The cabinets needed paint and the countertop was worn in places. The old range was chipped on the edges where dropped pots had hit. A burned spot on the countertop showed where a pan of burning peas was set without a trivet under it. The refrigerator was woefully small for a family of fifteen.

She nodded. "Heaven knows the kitchen needs updating. Can you manage the egg factory while I'm gone?"

"Of course. I'm an old hand at it. I'll get the chocolate eggs ready and we'll decorate them after you get back. You're going to miss your flight if you don't get going."

Easter gave her a long kiss before starting

toward the door. He paused before leaving, drew her into his arms, and held her like he wasn't going to let go. "I'll miss you." He pulled back and smiled.

Essie smiled back at him and waved him on to the garage. "I'll miss you too," she said, pushing a bench back under the table.

Having no time for more, she picked up her purse and followed the children outside. Strapping in all those children took a while, and they couldn't be late for the flight.

The good-bye scene at the airport was chaotic. The children filled the sidewalk as they helped their mother out of the vehicle and unloaded her luggage. The little ones cried as the older ones shouted at each other. Essie couldn't help but notice the passengers who sidled past the throng of children with a fearful look in their eyes. They were likely hoping this mob was not on their flights.

Essie took her time with each child, giving her full attention for a moment before moving on to the next. When the final good-bye was said, Easter pushed the children away and gave his wife a long kiss. Their children around them let out a hoot, drawing the attention of everyone in the departure zone. Embarrassed but flattered by her husband's passion, Essie smiled and told the children to get in the van. She took the handle of her luggage and pulled it inside the airport with the farewells still ringing in her ears.

Getting her ticket at the counter, she turned to look behind her. Only strangers were there. She felt very alone.

The line for security was long, but she made it through in good time. She dashed off to the restroom, the only place where she could get away from the crowds.

She dug in her purse for her lip gloss and found a small note folded neatly on top of her things. Pulling it out, she wondered what list she'd forgotten about. Unfolding it, she smiled when she saw Easter's handwriting. "Enjoy the freedom while you can. Come home soon. YLH."

A lilt was in her step when she exited the restroom. She was her own boss and was strong enough to face whatever might come.

Chapter 3

Sharon

A knock at the door brought Sharon Claus out of her kitchen inside her little stone condo on the frozen tundra of the North Pole. Wiping the flour from her hands, she opened the door for Elwin the elf who had a brown bag with him.

"Hello, Elwin! Come in. Thanks for bringing the mail. Want a fresh cookie?"

The heavy-coated Elwin wiped his mukluks on the entry rug. "No thanks, Mrs. Claus. The missus says I need to watch my weight. She says I've already put on my winter layer of flab." He laughed as he headed into an adjacent room which was her office. Her large, roll-top desk stood against one wall, and bookshelves with large books on them were on the opposite wall. He set the bag on the desk and took out the contents.

Sharon held the front door as Elwin headed back out into the cold. "Give Elwina my love," Sharon shouted as he climbed aboard his dogsled.

He waved his hand and gave the command to mush. Off he went in a cloud of white powder.

Martha the elf was in the kitchen cutting potatoes for supper. "Who was that?" she asked as she cut the Yukon goldens into chunks.

Sharon went back to the kitchen to finish kneading a batch of bread on the countertop. "Elwin bringing the mail. Nothing too exciting in it."

Later, Sharon left Martha with the baking and went to the home office to sort through the multicolored envelopes and packages of mail. Bills. Catalogs. Junk. A letter or two with Christmas lists that were way ahead of schedule.

At the bottom of the pile lay a letter addressed to her from a law firm in Sarasota, Florida. Sharon let out an exasperated groan. Lawyers usually sent their Christmas lists early, but it wasn't even Halloween yet. When would they learn Santa couldn't bring them a real Lamborghini?

The name on the envelope caught her eye. It wasn't addressed to Santa, but to her. This couldn't be good. Why would a lawyer be writing to her and not Santa?

Her heart started racing, and her breath came more quickly. With shaking hands, she tore the envelope open and spread the letter out in her hands.

Dear Mrs. Claus:

We regret to inform you that your mother, Francis Time, passed away of cancer on the 9th day of August.

The words burned her eyes. Her chin quivered as tears rolled down her chubby cheeks. She lifted a corner of her apron to dry her tears. A loud sob came out before she could stop it.

Her mother had passed and no one had told her about it. An unwelcome image of her mother dying alone in a hospital bed floated by her mind's eye. Her heart crumbled into her stomach. She hyperventilated, and her head started spinning.

Stumbling into the kitchen, she pulled a paper sack out of a drawer and started breathing into it. Martha rushed over to help, but Sharon waved her away. She went back into the office and sat in the large wooden desk chair. In and out the sack went until her head was clear, and she was once again in control.

Several minutes went by before she felt strong enough to finish the letter. Her father had handled the arrangements. A plane ticket was being furnished. She could travel to Florida to settle the rest of the estate.

Florida? Now? They were gearing up the toy factory for the push to Christmas. She couldn't leave now. She'd go after Christmas and take Santa along with her. He'd enjoy the vacation.

Looking back at the letter, she saw it was signed by someone named Howie Howard. A handwritten postscript at the bottom in the same handwriting as the signature offered to have a realtor present if she were interested in selling the house.

Sell her mother's house? Never! That was her childhood home. Her mother's home. No one else could live there.

A warm memory of sitting in her mother's kitchen filled her. Sharon could almost smell the ginger, nutmeg, and vanilla wafting in the oven-warmed air of her mother's kitchen. She and her sisters stood around the table, rolling out sugar cookies and taking turns using the cookie cutters to shape snowmen, reindeer, stars, and bells. The memories pushed a smile across her face.

Her husband's jolly voice came from behind her

as he walked in the door of the office. "I see by your smile that we are getting more letters from children."

His large belly hovered above her not-quite-as-large one as he looked at the letter in her hand. "They come earlier every year. Who is so anxious to send his list this year?"

Sharon showed the letter to Santa.

He stroked his long white beard. "That's not from a child. A law office! Another lawyer wanting a car or a new mansion?"

Sharon turned to look in her husband's twinkling eyes. Sometimes she wished they didn't twinkle so much. Not everything was worthy of a twinkle. She quickly looked down to hide her irritation.

She took a deep breath to calm her crossness. "It's not from a child, Santa dear. It's about my mother."

The jolliness dimmed a little in Santa. "You haven't heard from her for a while. How is she doing?" He looked at Sharon closely. "Is that a tear of homesickness I see?"

Tears spilled past the dam holding them back. In a shaky voice, she said, "I'm afraid she's gone. She died two months ago, and this lawyer—"she stood and faced her husband, " —is just now letting me know." The grief rained down her face as she cried on Santa's red undershirt.

Santa hugged his wife while she cried. "I'm sorry to hear it. She was a very nice lady. The world will miss her." He pulled a handkerchief from his pocket and handed it to her. "What can I do to help?"

Sharon gestured toward the kitchen. Her voice commanded rather than asked. "I was about to take lunch down to the workshop. Martha and I made sandwiches and cookies for the elves. Why don't you take them to the workroom so everyone can eat. She'll can help you with it. I need to be alone for a while."

Putting his thumbs under his suspenders, Santa said, "Yes, of course, dear. I'll take care of everything." He softly kissed her cheek as she left.

Sharon's steps were the only noise on the shiny tile floors in the hallway as she made her way to her bedroom. Hearing a pan hit the floor in the kitchen didn't slow her down or make her look back. She paused to shut the large wooden door, before rushing to the rocking chair near the window.

She looked out at the dimly lit sky. She wasn't aware of time passing as she sat there, her mind full of grief and memories of childhood. The last of the fall sunlight had faded when she blinked herself out of her trance and back to the present. She stood and looked out the window of her cozy home at the vast expanse of white reaching to the horizon.

Stars popped out in the late-afternoon sky. Soon the sun would be gone below the horizon for months, and darkness would fill the hours of the day. Inside, their large complex would be bright and cheerful—her favorite time of year.

The northern lights danced along the horizon, promising a specular show. The window pane where Sharon stood fogged with her breath, blocking her view of the moonlit, snow-covered land.

Her heart felt constricted, being squeezed by guilt and grief. While she hadn't been around her mother much during the past decade, knowing her mother was there comforted her. Without her mother,

her safety net was gone. Who would take care of her? A piece was missing from the jigsaw puzzle of her life. Her breath quickened, and her heart raced. Falling into a jittering abyss, she frantically searched for a paper bag.

Sharon was washing dishes in the kitchen when Santa came in from the barn after feeding the reindeer. She dried her hands and shed more tears on Santa's soft fuzzy coat.

He held her tight and let her cry, stroking her hair.

She wiped her face on his sleeve. "You know what the worst part is? The lawyer wants me to come to Sarasota to settle her affairs."

Santa pushed her away and looked at her resolutely. "You should go."

"But my sisters may be there, and you remember what happened at Hannah's wedding. Pandemonium!"

Santa rolled his eyes and nodded. "Who could forget?"

"People yelling and screaming. And that was before the wedding! How can I go through that again? Especially if you're not there!"

Santa shrugged. "I still say you should go."

Sharon started pacing and waving her arms to release her tension. "I can't! I'm not going." She crossed her arms and cocked her head, looking at Santa and waiting for him to agree with her.

Santa took a deep breath, as if summoning up courage to cross her. "Before you get too set in your decision, I think you should consider going." Santa held his hands up as if stopping a charging bull. "Hear me out. Go take care of business. Think of your mother.

Her wishes. The lawyer will likely read her will and you should be there."

Sharon stuck out her bottom lip a little as her resolve not to go wavered. She wanted to argue with Santa, but no words could be found to dispute his logic.

Santa took her by the shoulders and made her look at him. "It's been fifteen years since you've seen Essie and Hannah. Surely everything is behind you. Give them a chance to be your sisters again. Essie's husband is a real nice fella and Hannah, is she still married to the headless fellow?"

Sharon pushed him away and threw her hands in the air. "How should I know? I've heard nary a word from her or Essie all these years since that wedding. How can I face them? They're strangers to me now. I'm not going. Besides there's too much to do here. I have to start tracking who's naughty and who's nice."

Spinning around, she started washing dishes again. Santa came alongside her to help. His presence comforted her. She swirled the soapy water around a big pot, wiping it with a dishcloth.

Santa pulled a dishtowel from a drawer as Sharon rinsed the soap from the pot. He took it from her when she finished. "You know," he murmured, "you have to go. Your mother would have wanted it. She loved you. Go hear her last words in the will."

Sharon wiped the countertop as Santa wiped the pot dry. She was irritated with him because he was right. There was no denying it. She needed to be there when the will was read. Her mother would want that.

She threw the dish cloth back into the sink full of water and let out a sign of defeat. "You're right. I need to go. But it's such a bad time to leave. It's almost

Halloween which means people will start thinking about Christmas. Letters will start coming in. Who will sort the mail for you? And who will help you keep track of who's naughty and who's nice? That's my job!"

"Ho ho ho!" Santa laughed as he put the pot away. "Of course, no one can do it as well as you, but Martha will help. Don't worry about those things. Concentrate on getting matters settled."

Santa put his arm around her to lead her out of the kitchen. He paused to turn out the light as they made their way down the hallway. "Plan your trip. Settle your mother's affairs. Most of all, get reacquainted with your sisters. You'll probably find out they've missed you."

Sharon shrugged as she leaned against Santa's broad shoulder. "Maybe." She stood on her tiptoes and planted a kiss on Santa's cherry red cheek. "I'll go take care of things and come back as quickly as I can."

The next morning, Sharon sat on her bed in her spacious bedroom staring out the window at the twinkling stars. Clear skies meant frigid temperatures, and the bite of the cold was almost visible in the bright moonlight.

The trip to the small local airport would be a cold one, but living here at the North Pole, they were equipped for it. Her long velvet skirt hid her thermal wear, and her heavy velvet, fur-lined jacket would keep her warm. Her problem was she was headed to a place on the other end of the thermometer. She didn't have clothes for the beach.

Breathing too quickly, she tried to control it by

holding her breath as she turned away from the window. Martha, standing beside her, handed her a paper bag. Sharon thanked her friend and put it in her purse. She'd need it later, but for now, holding her breath was enough to slow the spinning in her head.

Wringing her shaking hands, she stared at her purse, plane tickets, and luggage on the bed, reminding her she was leaving her comfort zone for someplace she hadn't visited since she married Santa. Reminding her she had to see people she didn't want to see. And who probably didn't want to see her either.

Rummaging through her luggage again, she rearranged things and held up her one outfit suitable for hot weather. Even though it was lighter fabric, the long sleeves on the red flowered dress would be hot in the sun. She took it out of the luggage, then changed her mind and put it back. Changed her mind again and took it out.

Martha took it from her, folded it nicely, and put it in the luggage. She shook her finger at Sharon. "Zip it shut and forget about it. You're going to wear things out taking them in and out."

Sharon pulled the dress out again. "But it might be too hot with those sleeves. I should leave it."

Santa leaned against the door frame of their bedroom. "Take it. It looks good on you."

Martha refolded the long-sleeved dress and packed it in Sharon's luggage for a final time. She zipped it shut with flourish before leaving.

Sharon turned to Santa, waving her hands in nervous gestures. "I have warm weather clothes, but nothing for someplace as warm as Florida. I have one outfit, but I can't wear the same thing day after day."

Santa chuckled. "Wear your one outfit while you shop for beach clothes." He walked beside her and put his arm around her shoulders, holding out a credit card to her. "Merry Christmas! Go shopping with your sisters. It'll give you a chance to get to know each other again."

She looked at him sideways. "This isn't supposed to go in someone else's stocking, is it?" His twinkling eyes made her smile.

Santa shook his head as his belly shook with laughter. "It's an early gift from me to you. Enjoy!"

She gingerly took Santa's proof of permission to go shopping and stuck the card in her purse. She tried to lift her large suitcase off the bed, but couldn't.

Santa pushed her away and lifted it. With a soft groan, he put it on the floor for her. He stood erect and put his hand on his back.

Sharon eyed him closely. "You okay?"

Santa leaned backwards to stretch his back. He let out his usual trio of hos. "Of course! My toy bag is much heavier on Christmas Eve." Pulling out the handle, he wheeled the heavy suitcase out of the room. He muttered, "But not by much."

Sharon grabbed her purse, coat, and other things and followed him down the hallway. Reaching the front door, he helped her put her things down. "I wish you'd let me fly you down in my sleigh."

Sharon shook her head vigorously, leaving no doubt. "No! You've too much work to finish before Christmas Eve. I'll travel like everyone else does."

Santa shrugged and sighed in resignation. "Whatever." With a loving look in his twinkling eyes, he gave her a smile. "You look beautiful. Your sisters will be jealous of how young you look."

Sharon let out a groan. "My sisters. I'm afraid of what they will think of me. I'm much fatter than either of them. They'll laugh at me. Not to my face, but behind my back. I won't know how to act around them."

Flicking his hands like he was shooing flies away, he said, "Oh pshaw! Remind them of where we live. We need that layer of insulation to keep us warm. Haven't they ever seen seals and polar bears? Fat keeps them warm. Make sure they know the facts before passing judgment."

Santa started for the door, pulling the luggage behind him, but Sharon didn't move. Santa stopped at the door. "What's wrong?

Running to the chair by the desk in the office, she sat and buried her face in her hands. "I don't want to go. I want to stay here. Where I'm wanted. Where I'm comfortable. Where I'm loved." She cried softly into her hands.

Santa set the bag in the front door foyer before he shut the office door behind him. His knees popped as he knelt in front of his wife and pulled her hands away from her teary face. "Then stay home."

Sharon's head spun and her heart was racing as a heavy weight pressed on her chest. She was breathing as fast as her heart was beating. Dread consumed her completely.

Santa squeezed her hands. "Look at me. You're having an anxiety attack. Look at me, Sharon. Breathe slowly with me." He took in a slow breath and held it a few seconds before blowing it out. He repeated this as she followed his lead.

Her head cleared a little, and her heart slowed down as she got control of her breathing. Sharon kept wringing her hands, like she could wring her anxieties out of them. Her husband's reassuring touch brought her back to normal.

"I'm sorry, honey," she said. "I guess the stress of leaving is taking its toll on me. I don't want to go, but I know I should. But I *really* don't want to, but I know I *really* should. It's a never-ending cycle."

Santa groaned as he struggled to get off his knees and sat on the edge of the desk. "This trip is about your mother and her last request to you." He chuckled. "You might get a tan while you're gone."

"Or a very bad sunburn!" She was beginning to feel normal again and she was glad of it. She could finally think more clearly. "Mother didn't have a lot. We may need to sell her house. I want her rolling pin. I have many memories wound around it."

Nodding, Santa said, "Do what you think best after you get there." Santa started to leave, but stopped and turned back toward her. "The elves are waiting to tell you good-bye. Did you allow time in your schedule?"

Sharon smiled as she stood and straightened her outfit. "Yes, I wouldn't dream of leaving without seeing them."

Santa held out his elbow for her to take. "Come along, my dear. You're about to embark on a grand adventure, and they want to tell you good-bye."

Chapter 4

Hannah

Tapping her foot out of nervousness rather than to a beat, Hannah Horseman sat in a cushioned desk chair in her home office on her Pennsylvania farm. Pictures of horses hung everywhere above the rich carpet and polished wood furniture. Her husband, Headless, sat in his usual chair at the side of her desk, dressed in his favorite black leather pants with a black muscle shirt. His muscular form relaxed in the leather chair that fit his towering height. In this office and in these positions, they often discussed the business matters of their horse farm. But a letter held their attention now.

Hannah had sent their two sons, Horace and Huntley, out to water the horses so she could talk with her husband alone. Some business was none of their business.

Her hands shook slightly as she held a letter from Florida. She took a quick look at Headless who looked back at her with questioning eyes. His detached head sat on the cradle frame atop his shoulders. She'd fashioned the cradle from plastic ribs and cloth shortly after they met. Dressed in tall collars or a hoodie, he almost looked like his head was still attached. That allowed them to get out in public on rare occasions. Mostly, Headless preferred the solitude of his isolated farm.

The clock on the mantle clicked off the seconds as she stared at the letter. No use waiting any longer. Letting out a soft snort, she grabbed her letter opener and slit the flap with flick of her wrist.

Her hands shook slightly as she pulled the lawyer's letter out of the envelope and read the letter aloud.

> Dear Mrs. Horseman:
> We regret to inform you that your mother, Francis Time, passed away of cancer on the 9th day of August.

A cry of anguish escaped her lips, and tears clouded her eyes. She could read no more. Grief curled her hand holding the letter into a fist, crumpling the hurtful letter. Headless was at her side almost instantly, pulling her close as she sobbed. He took the letter out of her hand and read through the rest of it silently.

"Oh, darling," he said softly, "I'm sorry about your mother. I know how much you loved her. You should have gone to see her more often." He knelt beside his wife and offered his shoulder to cry on. She leaned on it, careful not to knock his head off its cradle.

Hannah reached for a tissue and blew her nose. She tossed the used tissue in the trashcan and reached for another to wipe her eyes. "After my sisters married and left home, we became close. Just the two of us, doing things together. How I miss those days!"

She cried softly for a few more minutes. Wiping

her eyes, she drew in a quick breath. "Did they have a funeral?"

Headless handed the lawyer's letter to Hannah. "It says your father took care of everything, but it doesn't say if he had her cremated or buried her somewhere."

"My father!" Hannah hurriedly looked over the letter, and raised her hands in exasperation as she crumpled it again. She flung it toward the trashcan. "Why didn't he call me? He should have let me know!"

She got up from her chair and paced around the office. "Did he tell my sisters?"

Headless retrieved the letter from its resting place and smoothed it out on the desk. Looking at the second page, he read off the carbon copy recipients. "Your sisters got the same letter as you did. I bet they didn't know either."

Grabbing the letter to see it for herself, she let out a growl. "Just as well. They probably don't care that she's gone." She crumpled the letter again, forming a fist around it.

She paced around the room, waving her hands as if grasping for an invisible answer in the air. "They never bothered to go see Mother. Sharon with her perfect little world at the North Pole. Said they were busy and she didn't have time to visit Mother."

She turned to face Headless who stood by her desk. "And Essie with her enormous brood. She wasted her registered nurse degree to become poor as church mice, and then had litters like they do. They would have to charter an overseas flight to go see her."

Pacing again, she tossed her head and said with

a voice dripping with superiority, "I'm the only one who went to see her with any regularity."

Headless stood behind a recliner and cleared his throat. "You haven't been there in three years."

Hannah stopped pacing. Had it been three years? Thinking back, she used her fingers to count the years. Her head lowered and her shoulders slumped a little. She'd lost track of time in the hustle and bustle of having two growing boys and their myriad activities. Now it was too late.

Tears flooded her eyes and spilled over. When she reached up to dry them, she scraped her face with the letter she'd forgotten she was still holding. She heaved a sigh as she smoothed it out on the table and folded it. She stuck it back into the envelope.

Headless came and put his arm around her small waist. "I'm sorry, honey. Losing your mother is a hard thing to deal with. The boys and I will help you through this." He held her tight as she cried.

After she'd cried it out, she went to the desk to get more tissues. "I guess that's that. Mom is gone." She wiped her nose and eyes.

"Not quite." Headless pointed at the letter. "It says there's an airline ticket for you."

Hannah ejected a loud ugh. "I can't go! Halloween is two weeks away. I can't possibly leave now. I have to get you ready to ride."

Headless wagged his finger in her face. "You have to go. What about your mom's cottage on the beach? You can't leave that hanging. Something needs to happen with it."

Hannah stared into space as the image of the cottage loomed before her mind's eye. That beloved cottage. One of the few places she felt completely at home. "My sisters will probably want to sell it and everything that's in it."

"And you're going to let them?" He looked at her with a glint in his eyes.

Hannah rubbed her temples, the pain of grief making the throb. "I don't want her ancient furniture. There's an old grandfather clock in there I'd like to have. It doesn't work, but we could get it fixed."

"So, you'd sell the cottage?" Headless said as he sat down in his leather chair. "That surprises me because you talk about the place a lot. You should hang on to it. You and your sisters could own it together. They could help pay the taxes"

She looked at her husband with narrowed eyes, and made him squirm in his seat. "I won't share Mother's cottage with my sisters. I despise them."

She walked in tight circles, flexing her fists like a fighter getting ready for a match. Her sisters! They, with their sweet, perfect husbands and high and mighty holidays. They always seemed to have little use for her and her physically disadvantaged husband and their unreligious holiday. They'd acted like they were better than she was.

She resented them for that and much more. Her sisters ruined her wedding day. She'd never forgive them. They shouted at her for choosing black as her wedding color. For inviting their ghostly friends. For marrying someone like Headless.

Essie had stormed off without staying for the ceremony or reception. Their mother was left in tears, trying to mediate peace between them all. Sharon stayed for the ceremony, but disappeared after that.

Neither of her sisters liked her or Headless. They said he was unlovable, and the marriage would never last. But she'd proved them wrong. She still loved Headless. He was a good husband to her and a great father to their two sons.

The creaking of leather as Headless rose from his chair pulled her out of her thoughts.

He came over to stand near her. "I can tell your imagination is taking over. Wait and see if there's going to be a fight."

Taking her hands in his, he uncurled them and held them against his chest. "Relax. Take it one thing at a time. Go back. See what happens. Maybe time has changed feelings."

"Humphf," Hannah snorted. "Not likely. And certainly not mine."

He waved off her response. "You owe it to your mother to go back and honor her life. It will likely be the last time you see your sisters."

Frustration and nervous energy started Hannah to pacing again. Her long hair hung across her face as she watched her feet follow the same path across the rug. "But what if they want to share the house?"

"Use your best judgment regarding the house. You have lots of happy memories being there. Your childhood sounded like a fairy tale. I wished I had had one so good."

Hannah's eyes and throat burned with sadness. Headless was right. She'd spent many happy years in the house, especially after her sisters left home and it was only her and her mother. Walking the beach, looking for shells, digging for clams, watching the clouds, and countless other things. All those things, she wanted her sons to experience. She could hang on to the house long enough for her family to spend Christmas vacation there.

Unable to argue with him, she signaled surrender. "You're right. I'll go, but I won't like it. I hate them, and I'll never forgive them for what they did at our wedding."

Headless leaned in close to her. "We should have eloped, like I wanted to. Then none of it would have happened."

She'd heard this before, and she didn't like it being thrown in her face again. She pushed him back. His head bobbled on the cradle, and she reached out to steady it. Guilt overtook the anger she felt toward him.

She threw up her hands. "We can't go back and change it."

He straightened his head. "True enough. Go and try not to make things worse—if they can get worse. Tolerate your sisters for a little while, just long enough to come to an agreement."

Feeling a little relieved at the thought, Hannah nodded. He was right. She only needed to negotiate what to do with the cottage. Surely, they could do that in a few hours. Afterwards, she'd be free of her sisters for good.

Headless lifted her chin. "The boys and I will manage Halloween if you aren't back in time."

Hannah patted his chest. It wasn't that she doubted it, but she hoped they'd miss her a little. "People will be disappointed if you miss your ride."

Headless pointed at her, emphasizing the words, "Nothing, and I mean nothing, will make me miss my ride. Don't you worry about that!"

Hannah pulled his head close to her and kissed his cold lips. "Thanks, Honey. I guess I should go talk to the boys."

She returned his head to the cradle and went looking for her sons. The youngest one was easy to find. He was playing with the new hellhound pups in the back yard. She called to him to join her in the house.

As best as she could, she explained what had happened, and that she'd have to leave for a little while.

"But when are you coming back?" Seven-year-old Huntley leaned against his mother's bed while she packed. "Why do you have to go?"

Hannah sat on the bed and motioned for her son to sit beside her. "Your grandmother—my mother—died. I need to go settle her affairs. While I'm gone, I need you to help take care of your dad and your brother. Can you do that?"

His big brown eyes stared at her, brimming with tears about to spill over.

She wondered if he was crying over losing his grandmother or about her leaving. At least twice, she'd taken her sons to visit her mother in the cottage by the ocean. He'd loved his grandmother's house. At the same time, she'd never been away from him, and he seemed scared.

She reached over and pulled him close as she rocked back and forth.

His bottom lip quivered as he asked, "Will Grandmother come back as a ghost like some of Dad's friends?"

Hannah's body stiffened involuntarily at the thought of her mother as a ghost. "I hope she'll rest in peace, Huntley. She deserves it, but if she comes back as a ghost, I'm sure she'll come see you."

A smile spread across her son's face. She knew he felt better.

"Don't you worry," she said as she stroked his dark curly hair. "Daddy and Horace will take care of you plus I'll ask Mrs. Hagg to come cook for you and watch after you."

Huntley jerked upright. "Her? She's creepy!"

"Don't say that! She's a good neighbor, and you don't talk like that about her." She looked closely at her son. He almost looked comical, with his lip stuck out below his furrowed brow and narrowed eyes. The corners of her mouth twitched as she suppressed the smile. "You be nice to her. Hear me?"

His face relaxed a little. "Yes, Mom. I'll be nice to her," he said with the voice of someone who had no choice. He dragged his feet as he left the room.

Hannah chuckled to herself. She agreed with Huntley. Mrs. Hagg was creepy looking, with missing teeth, thin gray hair, and a voice crackling like fire, but she had a heart of gold. Without children of her own, she loved Hannah's boys and would do anything to help. Hannah didn't care what she looked like. Mrs. Hagg treated her family with love and care.

Hannah finished packing her bag and went to find Horace, her 10-year-old son. He had always acted older than his age. She wasn't surprised to find him in his usual spot on a bench under the oak tree in the backyard reading a book. Sitting beside him, she let him finish reading before interrupting him.

"Hey, Mom," he said, putting his book down and putting a bookmark where he'd stopped. "When are you leaving?" His dark eyes stared intently at her as if drilling a hole in her mind to see in.

"In the morning." She put her arm around him and felt him tense in an I'm-too-old-for-this way. "I need a favor from you. Can you help with Huntley? He isn't too happy about my trip."

Horace released a groan. "Mmmmooommm! Can't you take him with you? He's so whiny and clingy. He doesn't listen to me when I tell him to go to bed or go take a nap." He shook his head vigorously. "Sorry, Mom, but I can't be responsible for him."

Headless walked up from behind the bench. "Yes, you can, young man."

Horace jumped at the sound of his father's voice and turned around to look at his dad.

Headless stopped in front of the bench. "Your mother asked you to do something and you're going to agree to do it. She takes care of you every day. She needs you to take care of your little brother while she goes away to take care of business."

A stern look from his father's head left no question about what Horace would be doing the next few days. He shrunk on the bench and looked at the ground. "Yes, sir. I'll keep an eye on Huntley." The low tone of his voice conveyed his disappointment.

"Good decision, son," Headless said as he started toward the house.

Hannah didn't want to leave Horace on such a harsh note. She spoke softly to him, "I know it's a hardship on you, and it will cut down on time with your friends and stuff. I'll be back as soon as I can get here."

He nodded without looking at her.

Her heart felt heavy. She couldn't leave him despondent. "I'll tell you what. Your grandmother had a nice library. What if I bring some of her books home for you?"

Horace thought for a minute before looking at her intently. He dug the toe of his shoe into the grass under the bench. "What kind of books?"

"Old ones. History books. Journals. Science. What do you want?"

Horace thought for another minute. "Whatever kind you think I'd like." He looked down at his book, searching for his spot in it.

Hannah watched his dark curls move in the breeze. He was a handsome boy who would be even more good-looking as a teenager. She felt her hand rise to lovingly brush his hair. He twitched his head in a motion that clearly said stop!

"Thank you for helping out," Hannah said to him before she ran to catch her husband, leaving their son to finish his reading.

The next afternoon, Hannah twisted in her narrow seat when the plane hit a little turbulence in the gathering afternoon rainstorms over Florida. A white-knuckle, infrequent flyer, she hoped this long flight would soon be over.

What was left of her diet soda sloshed in her plastic cup as another shudder hit the plane. She picked it up and quickly downed it so it wouldn't spill.

Her seat mate seemed unperturbed by the bumps. "This isn't bad compared to one flight I was on," the woman said. "One time we hit turbulence so bad, I was thrown out of my seat. Oh, honey, I nearly pooped in my pants." She laughed heartily at her statement. She looked at Hannah as if expecting her to respond in kind.

Hannah eyed the plump woman sitting next to her. "I hope it doesn't get that bad."

The woman's long, straightened hair surrounded a pudgy face too old for the hair style. Heavy makeup and long painted fake nails gave her the appearance of someone desperately clinging to the Hollywood image of youth. Hannah figured she was over 50, maybe more. It was hard to tell for sure, but then again, it didn't really matter.

Hannah raised her cup to fill her mouth with ice cubes so she wouldn't have to talk to the woman.

The lady patted Hannah's white-knuckled hand that had a death grip on the arm rest. "Listen, sweetie, this is pretty tame. Are you going to eat those?" She pointed at Hannah's little package of nuts sitting on her tray table.

Hannah's slightly queasy stomach quietly rumbled a request for food. She hadn't eaten since she'd left Pennsylvania early this morning, but the bouncing plane made the nuts look unappetizing. She pushed the bag toward the woman, hoping they would keep her quiet for the rest of the flight.

The woman grabbed the bag, ripping it apart. She poured a few into her hand and flung them into her large mouth with a backward toss of her head. Chomping them loudly, she repeated the action until the small bag was emptied.

Holding her head back as far as it would go, she dumped the last few crumbs into her open tater trap with gusto. "I love those nuts!" she exclaimed as she crumpled the wrapping and tossed it into her empty plastic glass. "What brings you to Sarasota?

"Family business." Hannah swirled the ice in her glass and looked out the window. Fatigue was starting to make her eyes heavy, and she leaned her head against the window, facing away from the woman.

"That usually means a funeral," the prying woman said. "Or reading of a will. Am I right?"

Hannah nodded slightly without taking her eyes off the passing ground far below. She crossed her arms and hoped the woman could read body language. The plane lurched again, and Hannah grabbed hold of the arm rests.

The woman patted the back of Hannah's hand again. "I'm sorry to hear of your loss." She cleared her throat. "Is there property you need to sell?"

She reached down under the seat and pulled out an enormous bejeweled purse and dug through it. Finding what she was looking for, she let out a quiet giggle of success and pulled out a business card. She held it out to Hannah. "I'm Elvira McKinzor, realtor and estate purchaser. I can help you with whatever you need done. I have a lawyer friend who can help with the legal mumbo jumbo involved. Can I make an appointment to see you after we land?"

Hannah looked at the Pepto-Bismol pink business card. Her queasy stomach wished for the real thing.

If she and her sisters decided to sell the cottage, they'd need a realtor to handle the paperwork. It would be nice to know what it was worth. An appraisal. That's what they needed.

She looked at the card again. Elvira McKinzor.

Hearing a light belch over the roar of the jet engines, she decided to never give her business, not even if she were the last realtor on earth. But she might have information that would be useful.

Hannah sat up straighter in her seat. "We may not sell it, but for curiosity sake, how much is a place on the beach worth?"

Elvira perked up more and played with the large beads of her long necklace. "Where is it?"

"At the end of White Sand Lane, west of Sar—"

Elvira yelled out, "A small stone cottage that sits right on the beach?" She turned as far as her tiny seat would allow her large frame to go and asked Hannah, "You mean the crazy woman's house? The one on the beach that sits on five acres?"

Hannah leaned away from the woman. "Crazy woman?"

Elvira cleared her throat and sat back in her seat as the plane hit another round of turbulence. "I—I'm sorry about that reference. I didn't mean it. Other people call her that, but I don't." She tapped her fingers on the tray top still holding her empty wine bottle, a plastic cup, and nut wrappers. "I'm sorry if that was your mother. I meant no disrespect."

Hannah looked out the window again. Crazy woman? People called her mother a crazy woman? She was the kindest woman she'd ever known. No one had the right to call her crazy. Anger boiled in Hannah like a teapot.

"I say again, sweetie, I meant no disrespect."

Hannah waved her hand in dismissal. The flight attendant came by and collected their trash. Hannah put her tray up, and leaned closer to the window, trying to get Elvira to quit talking.

Elvira leaned in closer to Hannah. "I could get you a good price for that place. I know lots of people who have been wanting to get their hands on that piece of property. It has a lot of potential. Not many other places have that much land with it. Yessirree bob, you could get a boatload of money for it. I'm the person who could do it for you too. Did I give you my card?"

"Miss McKinzor..." Hannah took a deep breath to squelch the anger enough to allow her to speak civilly. "It's not that simple. I have two sisters who must agree to this and I doubt they would accept any amount of money for their childhood home. They're very stubborn. It's quite impossible, but thanks anyway." She turned back to the window and softly bit her tongue, chiding herself for saying too much.

The captain came on to announce they would soon land. Hannah put her seatback up and tightened her seatbelt.

Elvira kept talking. "I'm sure I could persuade them to sell, if you'd give me their contact information..."

Hannah ignored her and looked out the window to see the ground getting closer. Soon she'd be able to escape this trap she'd made for herself and forget it.

Upon disembarking, Elvira followed Hannah down the concourse, talking the whole time. The faster Hannah walked, the faster Elvira talked although she was becoming more breathless with exertion.

At the exit from the security zone, Hannah saw a man holding a sign with her name on it. She quickly ducked through the crowd of travelers and turned the sign away, blocking it from Elvira's view. She hadn't told her her name and preferred to keep it that way. "Let's go," she told the startled chauffeur. "I have to get away from this lady."

The chauffeur took her elbow and directed her past the other people around them. He motioned to a security guard standing nearby. When the guard reached them, a single nod from the chauffeur directed him to Elvira who was still waving and yelling at Hannah.

"You have to go now, but I didn't get your number! I need to contact you later! Call me! You got my number!" Elvira kept looking back at Hannah as she was pulled by the guard down the hallway away from her. "Don't push me, I'm going."

"If you'll come with me," the chauffeur told Hannah. "The car is waiting. I'll take you to Mr. Howard's office."

Hannah breathed a sigh of relief and allowed herself to be led to the waiting limousine. Once inside, she splayed out, relieved to have lived through the flight and the harassment. The tribulation had already begun, and she hadn't faced her sisters yet. Somehow, she had to get through this. She tried to hang on to the hope that her sisters would be civil.

Chapter 5

Essie

Essie nervously paced the luxurious conference room of Mr. Howie Howard's firm, her flats mushing into the thick, deep carpet. She'd been the first to arrive, picked up at the airport by a chauffeur and limousine. Having never experienced first class service, she'd basked in the luxury.

A young, attractive secretary welcomed her to Mr. Howard's office on the eighth floor of a downtown building. Escorted to this plush conference room, Essie was told to make herself at home. Her sisters would arrive soon. After pointing out where drinks and snacks were, the secretary dismissed herself and left.

Essie wrung her hands a time or two while she surveyed the room.

A large, glass-topped conference table with ten chairs around it took up the middle part of the room. On one end of the room by the large window, a sofa offered a cozy place to sit and enjoy the view. On the coffee table were magazines showing the hot spots around town. The large picture window exposed the breathtaking view of Sarasota along the shoreline.

The blue of the water under the pale sky would have softened the heart of a normal person, but Essie saw little of it. Dread and fear ebbed and flowed inside her like the surf outside.

In the fifteen years since she'd seen her sisters, she wondered how—or if—they had changed. Would they get along better than the last time they met? Last time, there were tears, yelling, and insults so brutal the wounds were still raw.

Rubbing her chest as to lessen her heart's pain, she wondered if they could be civil to each other long enough to get through this. Their mother was no longer here to mediate between them.

Essie walked to the window and looked toward the sky, praying for strength. Since she was the oldest, the mantle of leadership fell on her, and as such, her mother's duties as mediator were squarely on her shoulders. Diplomacy was the best tactic.

The final matters should be simple. See if anything remained, find an equitable way to split it, and go their separate ways. Keeping her sisters focused on that instead of each other would make it go as smoothly as possible.

Feeling relieved at having a plan, Essie stood a little taller and smoothed her pale green A-line dress under its matching short sleeved jacket. She pressed her fingers over her chunky, bore-many-children figure under the mail-ordered outfit. If she'd kept those new year resolutions, she'd be wearing a smaller size to greet her sisters. The best she could hope for was they'd gained as much weight as she had.

The new flats bought to match the outfit were hurting her feet. She sat down on the end of the large sofa. Flipping her shoes off, she rubbed her feet. The massage calmed her nerves. Tired from her long flight from Germany, she took advantage of the sofa by stretching out on it. Her body almost melted into the soft cushions as her eyes closed.

The door made a whoosh as it swung open and the secretary walked in. Essie shot up from the sofa, kicking the coffee table with a loud bang. She quickly slipped into her shoes and stood, pretending she hadn't been caught by surprise in restful repose.

The secretary gave her a haughty gotcha look before stepping aside to reveal Hannah behind her.

Essie's stomach flip-flopped as she stared at her youngest sister. Her nose wrinkled slightly at the thin, ominous woman wearing all black. A tank top was under a black crocheted tunic that topped her leather pants. Her long black hair draped over her shoulders, straight and loose like the extras in an old vampire movie.

Essie felt the urge to roll her eyes, but managed to control the reflex.

The secretary pointed to the small refrigerator in the corner. "Help yourself to cold drinks and snacks. Mr. Howard will meet with the three of you when the last sister gets here." She paused another second, putting her hand on her hip and posing like a model in her girlish-looking power suit. Getting no reaction from the two sisters, she twirled as if on a runway and left.

Essie saw Hannah's eyes look her up and down, taking the whole sight in. The faintest hint of a smirk crossed her face before she walked to the window without saying a word. She didn't need to. Her high-brow look and the instant tension filling the air made it clear that nothing had changed in fifteen years.

Essie rubbed her forehead, trying to relieve the pounding dread and fear, both back with the full force of a hurricane. This was not going to be easy.

Thoughts whirled in her head like a queasy stomach churning. The words spewed out before Essie could stop herself from saying them. "I'd hoped you'd grown out of the dark phase of your life. Goth is out, especially at your age." The words went out like a lion on its prey.

Like a wild animal caught unaware, Hannah spun to face her attacker. "I didn't come here to be insulted. I'm here to settle Mother's matters and go home. Keep your rude comments to yourself." She turned back to the window and stared out. "Besides, you're no fashion plate yourself. You look like something out of Grandma's closet."

A gasp of shock spurted from Essie's throat. She looked down at her best outfit. The one she bought especially for today. The one Sylvie and Clara had helped her pick out. The one everyone in the family said made her look young and thin. Now, the polyester suit seemed cheap and ill-fitting.

Pulling the short jacket tight around her, she threw her head back. "I may not get my clothes from high-brow stores, but at least I don't look like the bride of Frankenstein." Biting her tongue in regret after the last barb, she crossed her arms and stared out the other side of the window, seeing nothing but her mind's anger.

Hannah stepped away and started pacing, mumbling lowly as she stomped on the carpet.

Too afraid to turn and look, Essie kept her face

to the window. This wasn't going as planned. She'd self-destructed in her role as peacemaker with her words.

Hannah grabbed one of the accent pillows from the sofa and whammed it against the sofa back.

The ferocity of the action made Essie take a step back, her heart pounding because she knew this angry outburst was of her making.

Hannah turned to her with eyes of fire. "Let's get through this so I can go home and never see or hear from you again, you—you arrogant rabbit!" She gave her sister one last fiery look before going to the other side of the room to sit facing away.

Regret swallowed Essie as the sting of the comment subsided. Hannah was right. It was none of her business how her sister dressed. But worse, Essie had failed miserably on the first test of diplomacy.

Guilt kept prodding Essie until it pushed out the reluctant words. "You're right. It was rude of me. I'm sorry."

Feeling her knees start to shake, she sat on the sofa and took a calming breath. "How have you been, Hannah? How are your boys?"

Hannah swung around and shot Essie a look with eyes like pools of magma. "Don't try to make up with me, sister. Anything nice out of your mouth is covered with poison. Keep it shut." She swung back around, slamming the door shut on any relationship between them.

Essie sat there, her mouth open with the shock of being stabbed in the heart. She didn't feel anything, being too stunned to realize what had happened. The pain increased, throbbing through her heart and into her brain. Her jaw wagged in efforts to say something in defense, but nothing came but squeaking sounds.

Suddenly, the conference room door opened, and the secretary came in again with Sharon in tow. Sharon walked toward her sisters with her customary smile and her mid-length red dress flowing behind her. Sharon, the forgiving, conflict-hating, always-cheerful, rotund sister, seemed ready to get along with her sisters. She embraced Essie warmly and gushed with sisterly enthusiasm.

As she approached Hannah, Hannah held out her forefinger, stopping Sharon in her tracks. A clear sign no hugging was allowed. Sharon stammered a greeting and retreated closer to Essie.

Essie frowned at the hateful-acting Hannah who didn't meet her stare.

The secretary let out an obvious snort and said, "Mr. Howard will be with you in a moment. There's water and pop in the refrigerator and snacks in the drawer beside it." She started out, but turned back. "Gluten-free snacks are also there," she added as she pointed at the refrigerator. She left the sisters on their own.

Sharon went to the refrigerator and pulled out a pop and took a package of crackers before sitting at the conference table. With sugar sweetness in her voice, she said, "It's good to see you both. We should get together more often." A pop and swoosh came with the opening of the soda can, followed by the sound of a crinkly wrapper being opened.

"You should stick with diet soda," Hannah said to Sharon who stopped chewing long enough to glare at her sister.

Sharon pulled her soda can closer to her and turned slightly with an air of defiance to shield her snack.

Essie sat by Sharon. "Leave her alone, Hannah." The two sisters squared off in a staring showdown while Sharon continued to crunch away.

Hannah sat down opposite of Sharon at the table. "The last time we were together, we hated each other. Nothing's changed. You made me cry at my wedding. That ruined my makeup and— "her voice grew in volume "—wrecked what should have been my happiest day."

Pointing at Sharon who was taking another drink from the soda can, Hannah continued, "And now you want to be a huggy sister? And you—" she pointed at Essie, "you think you have the right to criticize how I'm dressed, you oversized Easter egg! After this is over, we are no longer family You'll leave me alone. Forever!"

Essie winced inwardly. This meeting was turning out much worse than she'd expected. None of the wounds had healed. They were still raw and bare.

She blinked her burning eyes, determined not to let too many tears pool there. "I was out of line at your wedding, I admit it and I'm sorry. But can you blame me? I was shocked by the ghosts floating around. It scared me and set me on edge."

She took a deep breath while thinking of how to continue. If she dared. "Now that I'm older and wiser, I realize I may have overreacted. Do you think we can move beyond that day fifteen years ago?"

Hannah slammed her hand on the table and leaned across toward Sharon and Essie. "Never! You both called me an overgrown, clueless teenager. Told me I was too immature to get married to a handicapped person. That all I cared about was myself and being the center of attention. You said I wouldn't last a year with him."

Sitting back in her seat, Hannah looked at both sisters with smugness on her face. "Now what do you have to say? Headless and I are still in love, and we have two handsome sons and a wonderful life. Want to update your assessment of me?"

Having bent over backwards as far as she was willing to go, Essie felt Hannah's words fan the smoldering anger inside. Unable to control the inferno, Essie tilted her head so she could look at Hannah out of the corners of her eyes. "I've been meaning to ask, are your sons' heads attached to their bodies? Or are they loose like their dad's?"

Reflecting Hannah's posture, Essie felt self-satisfied, having asked the question no one else dared.

Infuriated tension filled the air over the conference table. Glares as hot as the surface of the sun passed between sisters.

Sharon choked on her snack, but quickly regained her composure. Throwing a bucket of water on the massive flames, she sputtered, "Ding ding ding. Back to your corners, ladies. We're here for a purpose. Let's at least respect each other. Or at least respect our mother enough to play nice together."

Hannah crossed her arms and sat back. "I respectfully decline to like either of you."

Sharon slammed her hand down on the table. "That's not what I meant! Oh, you make me so mad!"

Essie jumped in. "Forget it, Sharon. No sense in

arguing. Her heart's as black as her clothes."

Sharon turned on Essie like a guard dog. "You shut your mouth, you—you arrogant pastel-colored prig! You're the one who started this whole thing. You threw out the first insult at her wedding, and now you've insulted her sons. If you'd kept your high-brow opinions to yourself, we wouldn't be fighting about it."

Essie leaned away from Sharon's unexpected defense of Hannah. Her mouth opened to argue against the accusation when a plump man in a tailored three-piece suit swept the door open and came in like an emperor with his entourage.

An aura of arrogance surrounded the man like a swarming flock of vultures. A secretary and two paraprofessionals carrying file folders followed him in. The muttering of the followers left no doubt this was Howie Howard, their mother's lawyer.

He motioned for everyone to find a seat so he could hold court. He told the sisters to sit across from him. Moving their chairs away from each other as much as possible, they mutely observed a truce for the ceremony at hand.

The paraprofessionals gave Mr. Howard the folders they'd carried for him, and he took out a set of papers from one of them. Mr. Howard folded his hands and looked at the three women. "Your mother, Francis Time, asked that her heirs be together when her will was read which is why you were sent for. As you know, she died two months ago. At *her* request, this information was kept from you until I sent you the letters bringing you here."

He cleared his throat. "She knew you didn't get along and didn't want a fight between you three breaking out at her funeral."

Essie was stunned. A fight at her funeral? Is that what she thought of them? That they couldn't be affable long enough to attend her funeral? Her heart ached for her poor mother who must have felt alone, but was too afraid to call them to come. Her mother died alone. Alone.

The thought pushed tears out of her eyes and down her cheeks. She dug through her purse, looking for a tissue. The secretary slid a box of tissues down the table to her. She took one and wiped her nose.

Hannah took one too and did the same thing.

Sharon sat with her mouth agape and eyes fixed, as if in a trance. When Mr. Howard cleared his throat loudly, Sharon blinked back to life.

He looked through several pages while he said, "Your father was with your mother when she died. He left as soon as the memorial service was over, and we haven't heard from him since. Do you know where can we get a hold of him?"

As the oldest, she felt it was her responsibility to answer for everyone. "We didn't see our father often. He came around for a month or two and for Thanksgiving mostly. I have no contact information for him. Do either of you?" She looked at her sisters who both shook their heads.

Shrugging, Mr. Howard continued, "No matter. He's not in the will. It isn't necessary for him to be here. The husband not being named in a will may seem unusual, it's not unheard of."

He spread the papers in front of him and made preliminary remarks for the benefit of the record as his secretary wrote furiously. First, he read their mother's will that split her remaining assets equally between her three daughters.

Essie's heart sank, and she saw Hannah's head droop. Sharon gave Essie a quick look that showed her consternation. As much as they hated each other, the three of them were still bound together by their mother. Essie didn't know if her mother had a penny or a dime in her estate. The cottage was worth something. Hopefully enough to pay her mother's bills.

After reading the will, Mr. Howard shuffled the papers and patted them back into a neat stack. He slid the documents into one folder and chuckled. "Are these names for real? Hannah Headless, Sharon Claus, and Essie Bunny? What a hoot!"

He guffawed like a mule, his entourage joining in with him. He gave a signal, and they stopped laughing at once. "What's your legal names? You know, your real names?"

Essie felt her face burn with anger. "How dare you!" she said through clinched teeth as a stormy frown gathered on her forehead. "Those *are* our legal names. Don't mock them! It's unbecoming conduct for a professional man." She ripped the tissue in half, then didn't know what to do with the pieces.

One of the paraprofessionals handed her a wastebasket.

Embarrassed at her lack of control, she stumbled on, "We're here to settle our mother's estate and that, sir, is not a laughing matter. We need another, more professional lawyer to handle this matter." She glanced at her sisters whose frowns and furious eyes agreed with her. She stood.

Her sisters followed suit and stood.

Mr. Howard's smile was gone. He stood and apologized. "Please. No! I'm sorry! You're right. It was inappropriate of me. Please sit down, and we'll get this done as quickly as possible."

He leaned forward on the shiny conference table, staring at them with puppy eyes as if it would evoke sympathy for him. "Pleeeeeease," he pleaded with the voice of desperation.

Begging didn't become him, and Essie was repulsed. She looked at her sisters. Despite having little contact with them for so long, she knew what they were thinking. Get this done and over with.

She glared at the contrite lawyer. "I want my mother's estate handled with the utmost respect. She was a good woman and deserves no less."

"Of course, you're right. I apologize again. Please. Sit down, and let's finish the matter."

Sharon sat down first. Hannah slowly sat in her chair. They turned to look at Essie. A slight nod of Sharon's head encouraged her to do the same. After giving Mr. Howard one last glare, she took her seat.

"Thank you." Mr. Howard took out his handkerchief and wiped his brow. "Ashley, would you get water for our guests? And me."

As the young secretary pulled bottles of water from the refrigerator and passed them out, Mr. Howard continued, "Now, your mother was Francis Time, correct?"

The trio nodded their heads.

"And your father is who? He didn't introduce himself to anyone. I didn't get his full name. He came in and was gone quickly."

Through gritted teeth, Hannah spoke quickly.

"His name was Father Time. That's Mr. Time to you."

Mr. Howard's eyes grew large as he looked at each of the women, looking for a contradiction. His face reddened, and his mouth twitched with the desire to laugh again. He worked hard to muffle it as he waited for a corrected answer.

Getting none, he asked, "His *legal* name is Father Time? Was he a priest?"

"A priest?" Essie battled the urge to throw her water bottle at him, or a rock if she could find one.

Hannah had such a fiery look in her eyes Essie was surprised Mr. Howard's shirt didn't burst into flames. She spoke before Essie could, "No, he's no priest. He had a funny name like the rest of us. Going to make fun of that too?"

Tiny beads of sweat on Mr. Howard's forehead glistened in the fluorescent lights.

Essie liked how Hannah turned the tables on the irreverent lawyer and hoped peacemaker Sharon would keep her mouth shut. To make sure, she interjected, "You said our father didn't need to be here. Can we get on with this?"

Mr. Howard and his entourage were still stunned by the glare of Hannah. They looked at each other and bobbled their heads.

Mr. Howard shuffled papers and cleared his throat. "Of course. The deed to the house shows the three of you as owners so you can—"

"Wait!" Essie cried out. "All three of us? Are you sure? When did this happen?"

Mr. Howard looked quizzical as he shook his head. "Your mother had me do that several years ago. Told me you'd each paid one dollar for it."

Sharon gasped and said quickly. "Oh, yes! I remember now. Don't you two?" She looked at each of her sisters with raised eyebrows and pleading eyes.

Hannah coughed and squirmed in her seat. "Oh yeah! I remember too. I'd forgotten about that. I'm glad you reminded me, Sharon. How about you, Essie?"

"How could I forget. I recall sending her a dollar for the cottage."

Essie took the paper from Mr. Howard and studied the deed to the oceanside cottage. The sisters' names were listed as owners of the property, like he said. The date showed they'd owned it for the last three years.

Her dreams of a new kitchen were sinking as she passed the deed on to her sisters to look at. How would she ever get them to agree to sell the place?

Mr. Howard sat back in his chair and tapped his fingertips together. "You three own a desirable place near the beach. I assume you'd consider selling it since none of you lives here. From what I heard through the door before coming in, you don't get along with each other. I can get you a good deal for it if you sell it."

He leaned forward and uttered in a greed-saturated voice, "A *very* good deal."

He sat back, a self-satisfied look on his face. He twisted his large diamond ring around his finger, waiting for them to react.

Essie looked at her sisters. Hannah looked like she didn't trust anyone in the room. Sharon was still and pale. Essie couldn't decide what they were thinking of his suggestion. She wanted the money, but to sell her beloved childhood home to this ruthless, self-seeking man seemed like an abomination.

She pulled the deed to the cottage closer to her. "We'll have to talk about it. Is there anything else we need to do? Did she have other property or bills needing to be paid?"

Mr. Howard shook his head as he opened another manila envelope lying in front of him and pulled out a set of keys. "All of her bills have been paid. As far as we could find, the house and its contents were her only assets other than a few thousand dollars in the bank that an accountant is tracking. She had no debt. Everything, including funeral expenses, has been paid."

He handed the keys to one of his assistants who put them on the table in front of Essie. "There are the keys to your house."

"Are we done here?" Hannah picked the keys up and put them in her purse.

"Ye—"

Ashley nudged the lawyer and whispered in his ear.

"Oh yes, I almost forgot."

He fumbled with another manila envelope and pulled out a letter. "Your mother left a letter to be read in private when you were together. I haven't read it—" he laughed out loud "—she made me swear that I would leave it unopened. You can see that the seal on it has not been broken."

He waved the envelope in the air. "If after you read it, you need my services, call me. Even real estate services. No sense in paying a realtor to do what I can." He let out a greedy huffing sound Essie guessed was supposed to be a laugh.

"I recognize Mother's handwriting," Sharon said

as she took the letter and lovingly caressed it as if she could feel their mother's hand there. "We should let Mr. Howard read it to us."

"We'll read it after we get to the house," Essie said, still staring at the envelope.

She felt her stomach shrivel into a knot. Why did her mother leave the house to the three of them? She knew they weren't on the best of terms. Was this her way of forcing them to negotiate an armistice? They'd need one if they were going to share the cottage.

Mr. Howard cleared his throat with gusto, sounding like a gavel hitting the judge's bench. "And with that, ladies, this concludes our business. Remember, if you want to sell the place, I can get a big pile of money for it. I'll take care of the paperwork and you'll be on your way in no time."

He looked at them with open hands, inviting them to make a decision on it now. "I guarantee you a really good price for it." He wagged his fingers to encourage a positive response.

Essie shook her head slightly, and watched as the spark left his eyes.

He threw up his hands and motioned for his entourage to get ready to leave. As his party stood and started toward the door, he said, "I took the liberty of getting you a rental car. My secretary will show you where it is and give the keys to you. Good luck. You have my card."

Mr. Howard stood and shook their hands and left with his stoic followers. The secretary stayed behind to show them the way out.

Out in the rental car, Sharon sat in the front seat, holding the letter tightly to her chest like a precious treasure that might fly away, while Essie pulled out of the parking lot and onto the unfamiliar road. The car's GPS unit called out directions as she drove.

Years had passed since they'd been there, and the town looked a lot different. The traffic was heavier than Essie was used to driving in. With a white-knuckle grip, she maneuvered the car safely down the street.

From the back seat, Hannah yelled at Essie to turn and Sharon would yell not to turn while the GPS unit stayed silent.

Essie was a nervous wreck trying to follow their conflicting directions and safely drive in the heavy traffic.

Eventually they found themselves on the edge of town, going in what seemed to be the right direction. With increasingly familiar landmarks and mounting fatigue, hostility between the three eased as they made their way down the driveway to their mother's cottage by the ocean.

Chapter 6

Sharon

Beach sand was like ball-bearings under the sisters' feet as they went up the steps and across the large front porch sheltering the front door of the cottage from the noonday Florida sun. The whitewashed house was full of memories, waiting to spill out as soon as Sharon opened the door. The porch swing swayed back and forth, inviting her to sit on it. The sound of the surf and the rustling of the wind through the grass took her back in time, and she could almost hear her mother's voice in the breeze.

Sharon opened her eyes when the door creaked open. The breeze rushed past the sisters and into their childhood home, ruffling the lace tablecloth under the brass lamp on a marble-topped end table.

While most of the room still had the Victorian style furnishings as before, in the middle of the living room was a modern leather recliner sofa with a matching overstuffed chair. The eclectic mix of furnishings faced the extra-large TV atop another marble-topped table. The leather furniture and flat screen TV looked out of place surrounded by furniture at least 100 years older.

The hallway leading to the bedrooms was on the left. The kitchen to the right was as Sharon remembered it, with an eating bar and enough cabinet space for a well-stocked kitchen. Here was her favorite room in the house. Here her mother taught her to bake, a legacy that lived on at the North Pole when she cooked for the elves and Santa. If the fighting between her and her sisters got too bad, she would find sanctuary here.

Later, she'd take inventory and make a list of things to buy. Essie could go get groceries for her. Santa might not have meant for her to buy ingredients with her gift card, but if it meant saving her sanity, he'd understand.

The sound of a soft-spoken conversation brought her out of the kitchen. Essie and Hannah were looking at the old grandfather clock by the brick fireplace. The rich wooden case had leaves and flowers carved around the outer edges of the rectangular clock face. The yellowed face had large numbers with gold-leaf interiors. The gold pendulum hung still behind the long glass door. The hands showed it was nine-fifteen. Like they always had.

Sharon turned around, taking in the scene inside the cottage. "Unusual style of decorating. Modern with the old. Everything is still neat and clean. It's like she went to the grocery store and will be back any minute. I still can't believe she's gone." Her hand went to her quivering chin to steady it.

The house seemed dead. Everything was in its place and looked the same, but the spirit of the home was gone. The house, once alive with laughter and love, was now a shell. Her mother was gone, taking her vibrant spirit with her.

Essie and Sharon surveyed the house while Hannah stood motionless in front of the clock. Various knickknacks covered the shelves hanging on the wall, all of which were dust free.

Essie ran her finger across the top of the coffee table in front of the sofa and rubbed her fingers together. "How could it stay this clean after two months of no one living here?" she said. "No grit or dust. It's had a good cleaning recently."

Sharon went into the kitchen. Her shoes squeaked on the clean tile floor. Opening the refrigerator door, she found it stocked with milk, eggs, orange juice, and the usual items needed for everyday living. She checked the expiration date on the milk. It was good for another week. Someone must have left the kitchen stocked for their arrival.

Her heart racing with creepiness, she called out, "Something strange is going on here. There's food in the kitchen. Fresh food." Her sisters came up behind her to look in the refrigerator with her.

"That *is* strange," Essie said. She went to the back door to check if it was locked. "Burglars wouldn't leave the place this neat. Must be someone else."

"Mr. Howard probably had it stocked for us," Hannah said as she surveyed the refrigerator contents.

Essie opened a cabinet that held a good stock of canned goods and held the door open for them to look in.

The kitchen delighted Sharon, making her heart feel light. "At least, he's useful for something. I'm hungry. Let's eat!" She reached into the cabinet and pulled out a loaf of bread. "There's lunch meat and tomatoes and lettuce and mayo in the refrigerator. There's also apples and bananas on the counter."

Hannah let out an exasperated growl. "We're home for the first time in fifteen years and all you want to do is eat?" She spread her arms wide in Sharon's direction. "Of course, why am I surprised? Look at you! You obviously enjoy your food."

Sharon was stunned into paralysis. For a few minutes, she'd forgotten about their feud. It had come roaring back to life. She threw the bread onto the eating counter, not knowing how best to release her inner distress. Should she sob? Or should she roar like a hungry polar bear ready to kill?

Essie calmly reached into the refrigerator and got a jar of mayonnaise and a package of deli meat. "Sharon's not the only one hungry here. I didn't have much breakfast. So, Miss Skinny Bones, mind your own business while we eat. Any cheese in here?" She turned her attention back to the refrigerator while Hannah stomped out of the kitchen in a huff.

Sharon grabbed a paper towel and dabbed her eyes. The confrontation sprouted a huge lump in her throat and had taken away her appetite. She whimpered, "Why can't we get along? Even for a little while? Why do we hate each other so much?" As hard as she tried, she couldn't hold it in any longer and morphed into a blubbering mess.

Essie put cheese and mayonnaise onto the table and opened cabinet doors looking for plates, seemingly oblivious to Sharon's pain. "I don't know. We're different. Very different. And none of us wants to give in to the others. We end up butting heads." She put plates and silverware on the eating bar. "I wonder if there're any chips?"

Sharon watched her nonchalant sister set two places at the eating bar and open the lunch meat and bread. Wadding the damp paper towel, she flung it into the empty garbage can. No sympathy or comforting word came her way.

Food was Sharon's comfort for her aching heart, and she needed a lot of it to soften that amount of hurt. Letting out a sigh of resignation, Sharon joined Essie as she opened a bag of potato chips. Nothing was said between them while they ate.

After lunch, Sharon opened the door to her childhood bedroom. She rolled her luggage in, and stared at the room. It was as she remembered. A small bed was against one wall, and a chest of drawers was across from it. A mirrored bureau was on the other wall beside the closet door. Even her color scheme was still there. Blue. Like the sky and the water.

She loved blue. She looked down at her red dress. She wore red because Santa loved her in red. All her clothes were red. She wanted to take off her red dress and wear something blue. She opened the closet and looked in. Empty hangers were the only things occupying the space.

She lay on the bed, glad to finally be alone. She put her arm across her eyes, trying to block out everything around her. Imagining she was a girl again, she yearned for her mother to come in and comfort her.

So much had happened in the last twenty-four hours. Her head cascaded with stress, fear, and questions. She needed her mom to come in to tell her everything was going to be all right.

The longer she lay there, the stuffier the room got. Feeling like she was going to break out in a sweat, she got up and took off her long-sleeved dress and put on her slacks and a short-sleeved undershirt, the only things she had to wear appropriate for Florida's temperatures.

The urge to go shopping hit her. She wanted a blue dress, one that was long and flowing. One that was light enough to let the cool ocean breeze flow through it. Surely there was a dress shop somewhere in town with clothes in her size. She had Santa's gift in her purse, waiting to be warmed by a scanner. She could take the car and go back to town. So what if she hadn't driven a car in quite a few years. It would come back to her. Like riding a bicycle, only more dangerous.

She opened the drawers of the bureau and found a hair brush. She studied herself in the mirror. She was wider and chunkier than she visualized herself being. Her hair was almost completely white.

Perhaps Hannah was right. She'd let herself go somewhat. A long walk on the beach would help her grief and her apprehension of being with her sisters. And it would be good exercise. She needed sandals for that. A shopping trip was what she needed.

She turned away from the mirror and surveyed the room again. Funny how her mother never changed anything. The room was like a time capsule being reopened years later. She and Santa had been married almost twenty-two years. In that time, her mother had never turned her bedroom into a craft room or a reading room or storage place. Or anything useful for a woman with an extra room. She'd already turned her son Sam's room into her private office.

Essie's voice from the living room disrupted her thoughts. "Anyone want to read Mother's letter with me?"

Sharon rolled her eyes. Essie yelled rather than walking down the hallway to make a request. She yelled back, "Be there in a minute!" as she hung up her red outfits. It was time to reenter the fray.

Essie was sitting on the sofa with the envelope Mr. Howard had given her on the coffee table in front of her. Still dressed in her dress clothes, she looked stern, her lips pressed tightly together like she was keeping something from spilling out.

Hannah was in the overstuffed chair, her legs drawn up under her. She'd already changed into something more casual. Her black leggings were covered with a black tunic with a sequined skull on front.

Sharon sat on the other end of the sofa from Essie, not giving her a glance. She might lose control of her anger if she looked at her critical sister.

Hannah unfolded her legs, repositioning them. Out of the corner of her eye, Sharon saw Hannah's foot moving vigorously as if something inside was fighting to get out. Her restlessness was contagious, causing Sharon to shift in her seat. Uncomfortable with the heavy silence, she was about to leave the room.

"I'm sorry about what I said to you in the kitchen, Sharon." Hannah sounded more nervous than regretful. "I was out of line." She quit twitching in her seat. The release of her thoughts must have stilled her nerves.

Sharon sat still, wondering if she'd dreamed it or if she'd heard right. She gave a quick glance at Hannah who was looking at her hands. A heavy sigh escaped her, releasing some of her stress. "Apology accepted."

Essie, ever the boss, closed out the moment. "Girls, we're stuck here for a day or two. Somehow, we need to put aside our differences and try to get along. We don't have to like each other, but we need to be amenable. It's the only way we can get this done. Afterwards, we'll go our separate ways, never to meet again. Can we call a truce in the battle?"

"Truce," said Sharon, echoed by Hannah.

"Good," Essie said as she snuggled into the sofa. "First, let's get reacquainted a little. Hannah, how are your boys?"

Hannah paused so long she wondered if she'd get a response at all.

Panic filled Sharon's chest. The truce would never work.

A slight smile crept across Hannah's face. "The boys are great." Her voice held a mother's undying love. She curled her legs back under her, a far-off look in her eyes. "They're growing so fast I can barely keep them in clothes. And how are your children? How many are there now? I can't keep track of the brood."

Sharon saw Essie grit her teeth and close her eyes. She did the same. Their mother would have wanted them to be nice to Hannah even when she wasn't nice to either of them. She held her breath to quell the rising panic, waiting to see if the shaky truce would hold or not.

Essie opened her eyes and put a pleasant look on her face. "I have thirteen children. Dinnertime around the feeding trough gets pretty chaotic. It's like living in a nest of birds. They have their mouths open, and I go by and drop something in."

That did it. A soft laugh came out of Hannah and a bigger laugh came out of Sharon. Peace had been restored and the truce was intact.

Sharon felt a jolt of happiness flash inside as she admired the first smile she'd seen on Hannah's face since before the wedding. Disregarding her attire, she could see how pretty Hannah was, almost like a model. Time had been kind to her.

Sharon took the conversation a step farther. "And how is Headless?"

Another faraway smile softened Hannah's face as she looked Sharon square in the eye. "He's good. He and the boys are taking care of the horses. The boys have taken a big interest in them. After school and homework, they're usually in the barn brushing and working with the horses."

Essie adjusted her skirt. "How nice they are focusing on the family business. I've tried to get our oldest children interested in helping at the egg factory, but they don't seem to care about it. I'm worried about who will help Easter after I am gone."

Hannah's eyebrows went up. "Out of thirteen, there's bound to be someone who will take over. At least the odds are with you." Hannah turned to give a slight smile at Essie who returned the smile.

Essie turned toward Sharon's end of the sofa. "And how's Sam, Sharon?"

At the mention of her son's name, Sharon felt her face crinkle into a smile. "He's in his first year of college. I miss him, but he's having the time of his life. He thinks he'll major in business and marketing which we hope means he'll help Santa when he graduates."

Sharon stopped, afraid. "He hasn't said for sure. I mean, we assumed — "

Essie waved her concerns away. "Don't think about that now. There's time to persuade him." She reached out and patted Sharon's knee.

Sharon's thought left Sam and went to feeling her sister's reassuring pat. It felt good! She wished her mother was there to see it.

Their tenuous truce was holding for now. Without that, they'd scratch each other's eyes out.

Chapter 7

Hannah

Sitting in the overstuffed chair, Hannah pulled her long thin legs up under her. She leaned against the overstuffed arm and made herself comfortable. Sharon sat near the end of the sofa and put her bare feet on the coffee table.

Years of training by her mother echoed through her thoughts. Putting feet on the table was strictly forbidden. On impulse, she couldn't let it go. "Put your footrest up, Sharon, before Mom comes back to tell you to get your feet off the table."

Sharon gave Hannah a quick flash of ire in her eyes before she complied with the instructions.

"Get your feet off the chair," she growled back. "Mother didn't like anyone's feet on the furniture."

Hannah felt the sourness of having to eat her words. It lit an annoyed anger inside. She uncurled her legs and put the foot rest out with a harsh bang.

"You two sound like my kids," Essie said as she opened the letter from their mother.

The words were like a bellow on the fiery anger already glowing inside Hannah. Her hands went to the arms of the chair to push her up. She wouldn't sit here any longer if insults were going to be traded.

With a dramatic wave of her hand, Essie tore open the letter from their mother. "Let's see what Mother has to say."

Her mother's memory doused Hannah's anger, and she lowered herself back into the soft confines of the chair. Closing her eyes, she took a calming breath.

Essie started reading:

My dear girls:

When you read this letter, I'll be gone. I know you'll be shocked I didn't let you know, but I didn't want a bunch of prattling around my death bed. I'm not afraid of dying. I'm an old woman and it's my time.

In the hall closet, I've left my last wishes recorded on a video. Find it, and listen to it. Don't go home until you do. It will explain what I need you three to do for me. I'm not asking too much of you, my daughters. Only that you grant me my final wish.

I signed over my house to the three of you. Share it. It's a wonderful place to vacation or to live. Work it out amongst yourselves. Never sell the house. Trust me, girls, you won't regret it.

This house is not only full of happy memories, but also full of magic. Yes, girls, magic! The old grandfather clock by the fireplace is a special clock. A powerful clock. In time, you will discover its powers.

I've left the instructions to the clock on the video. Before you start watching the video, set the clock dial to five o'clock and give the pendulum a nudge. Trust me, it will work. I'll leave it to you to discover the magic of the clock and what it will do for you.

The clock only works in the house. It's imperative you keep it. Again I say, never sell the house.

Even though we haven't seen each other in years, you've been on my mind all the time. I have always loved you three and always will. You have wonderful, kind, loving husbands. You love your children and are raising them to be good people.

I am proud of the three of you for seeing children everywhere have a special time on the holidays. Your hearts are large enough to love those around you. See if you can't open your heart to each other too.

Good-bye, my darlings, until I see you again. Please remember me as I was when you were girls and the fun times we had together in our happy home by the ocean.

Love, Mom

Hannah sat silent, stunned so deeply she was numb. The words Essie read had come through in her mother's voice, speaking to her heart.

Her mother said she loved her and was proud of her. Nothing gave Hannah greater joy than to hear it. Her grief was eased by the words.

Her mother held no grudges, but loved her and her sisters despite getting caught in their feud. Her mother was proud of her sons-in-law, and that must mean Headless, and her grandchildren. And that love lived on.

The sound of low sobbing made Hannah blink out of her trance. Her fingers moved past her cheek and came away wet. Looking for a tissue, she sniffed and wiped her other cheek with her hand.

Sharon took a tissue out of a box and pushed it down the coffee table. As the box went by, Essie picked one out too. With a soft nudge, the box stopped in front of Hannah.

Hannah gave a slight nod in thanks. Blowing her nose made her feel a little better.

Essie blew her nose and announced in a shaky voice, "Let's go find that video so we know what's special about a clock that doesn't work."

Sharon followed her into the hallway.

Hannah didn't move. It didn't take three people to get a videotape from the closet. A video! Their mother was never one to keep up with technology. She scanned the machines under the large TV. A machine with the old flip slot was there, and she let out a breath of relief. They were in luck.

A screech rang out from the hallway. Hannah went to join Essie and Sharon in staring at the mess in the closet. It was crammed full of videocassettes. Row upon row and tier upon tier and not one spine had a label on it.

Desperation filled her. She pulled out several and looked for labels on the front. They all looked the same. Black cases with no labels. She pulled more out with the same result. Their mother had left them a closet crammed full of unlabeled videocassettes.

Throwing down her armful of cassette tapes, she threw up her arms. "How are we supposed to find which one tells us about the clock? I don't have time to watch all these! Halloween is only two weeks away and I have to be home before then."

Kicking one of the cassette tapes, she let out a growl. "This is ridiculous! What was Mother thinking? Is she tormenting us for not coming home more often? You watch them! I'm going home!" She stormed back into the living room. Too upset to sit, she marched in front of the TV like a sentry on guard duty.

She came here thinking she'd look the house over, then leave for home. Now this. Halloween was the biggest day of the year for Headless. She wouldn't let him down by sitting here watching videos, searching for one her mother insisted they watch.

But if she left now, her sisters would have the house and their mother's instructions. As much as she loved Headless, she couldn't let her sisters have one thing more than they already had. She was part owner of this house, and she was going to stay to make sure her sisters didn't jump her claim. What to do. What to do. What to do.

Sharon's voice rang from the hallway, "Which one do we start with?"

Hannah could hear her rustling around the videos. Remembering the videos she'd dropped on the floor, she wondered if bossy Essie would make her come pick them up. The sound of popping knees drifted into the living room. Someone else was taking care of that chore.

Essie had three in her hands as she walked back into the living room. "This one is as good as the next."

Sharon came in, her arms filled with videocassettes. She dumped them onto the coffee table. "Mother wouldn't do this to us intentionally. There's got to be a reason why she did this."

Essie stood with her hands on her hips. "I agree with Hannah. This is her punishment for not coming to visit more often." She sat on the sofa. "I'm guilty of it. I haven't been here since before the wedding."

Sharon sat in her place on the sofa. "Me neither.

We are busy year-round. I never took the time to come."

Hannah continued to tromp in front of the TV. "I came more often than either of you. Why is she punishing me too? Why should I suffer because you two were negligent?"

Essie puffed up like an adder. "Negligent! Aren't you high and mighty about it. I wanted to visit, but couldn't. You may be able to afford fifteen airline tickets, but I can't."

Hannah made a face. "I forgot. You and litter can't go anywhere."

Essie jumped up from the sofa. "Don't you dare insult my family!" She started around the coffee table toward Hannah.

A loud screech came from Sharon. She held her head and rocked back and forth. "I stand it anymore." Her voice was shaking, along with her whole body. "The conflict. The hatred. The yelling." She broke out into an ugly crying jag.

Hannah looked at a deflated Essie who stared at Sharon with sad eyes. She felt the same way. Hannah looked at her mother's and father's portrait on the wall. She couldn't stay mad at her mother for long. She was gone, leaving behind a simple request. Listen to a video with instructions on it. She didn't intentionally inconvenience her. It just happened.

Putting her face in her hands, Hannah muttered, "You're right, Sharon. The better we get along, the faster this will go and the faster we will get home."

Sharon's broad waist broadened more with a sigh as she dried her tears. "Mother wanted us to be here together. Like it or not, we're stuck. I want to go home too, but if I have to stay to find this video, you do too."

Hannah bit the insides of her cheeks and took a deep breath. "Okay. We've got a chore to do and limited time to get through it. We should do this in shifts. One of us watches around the clock until we find whatever video she wants us to find. We can fast forward through what's on there, looking for one where she's speaking to us. It may not take as long as we think it will."

Essie went to the TV stand and turned the VCR machine on. After inserting a videocassette, she rummaged through a pile of remotes looking for the one that ran the TV. She tried one by pushing a button, but nothing happened. She pushed it again, using both thumbs on the button. Still nothing.

With a loud wham, Sharon put her footrest down and stomped over. She took over the chore.

Hannah went to the overstuffed chair to sit. If she tried to help, another argument would break out. Emotional fatigue convinced her to sit this one out.

Sharon collected the remotes and set them on the table. Examining them, she held one up. "You got the wrong remote!" She hit a button and the TV screen came on, showing a news program from somewhere.

Playing with the remote a little more, a whirring sound started. The screen turned black and blinked several times before turning to static. Sharon hit the pause button on the remote which stopped the video. She gave a smug smile.

Essie let out a grunt of exasperation. "Smart aleck!" When the TV went blank again, she shouted, "See! You don't know what you're doing any more than I do! Let me try again!"

Hannah cringed as she watched her sisters wasting time as they fussed with each other over how to work the ancient machine. She had no time for this bickering. Her boys needed her and so did Headless, especially with Halloween rapidly approaching.

A bolt of panic went through her. She'd forgotten to take his Halloween-ride ensemble to the cleaners! His cape was wrinkled and needed cleaned and pressed. Pulling her cell phone from her pocket, she dialed home on her cell phone and soon Horace answered.

"How are you, son?" Her voice sounded more strained than she wanted to admit, but hoped he wouldn't notice.

"I'm fine, Mom. Is something wrong with you?"

Hannah cleared her throat. "Just a frog in my throat. I'm fine. I need a favor. I forgot to take your dad's Halloween clothes to the cleaners. Could you ask Mrs. Hagg to do it for me? He needs them for his ride."

"Can I write her a note and leave it on the table? I don't like talking to her. She's so—"

Hannah could tell he was struggling not to worry her or get into trouble for what he wanted to say.

"—hard to look at and talk to. Can't Dad take them down?"

"Now, Horace, you know your dad doesn't like getting out right before Halloween. It spooks people."

"I know. Okay, I'll ask her to take his stuff down."

"You won't forget, will you?"

"No, Mom."

"How's Huntley?"

Horace moaned. "He's a whiny brat! He keeps asking when you'll come home. I told him never if he didn't quit his whining."

Hannah closed her eyes, trying to block out her sisters' continuing quarrel over the remotes. "Horace, you know better than to tell him that. You tell him I love him and I'll be home as soon as I can."

"Okay, Mom," he said in a do-I-have-to voice. "So, when are you coming home?"

Hannah smiled. Her oldest son had betrayed his feelings. He wanted her to come home. The loud sounds of Essie and Sharon fussing interrupted her thoughts of home. "Not soon enough, Horace. I have to go. Tell Huntley and your dad I called. I miss you all!"

Hannah bit her bottom lip to keep it from trembling as she hung up. She folded her arms and glared at the backsides of her sisters as they argued over the VCR operations. The urge to kick them in their rumps was almost too much to hold back.

Essie had two remote controls, one for the TV and one for the ancient VCR machine. Sharon kept grabbing for them, but Essie would move them out of her reach.

Sharon punched the buttons on the front of the machine. The effect was an increase in volume of the argument.

After a few choice words spoken by Essie that Sharon rebuked her for, a fuzzy picture of their mother appeared on the screen. It flickered a little, flashing images of different times and recordings, but finally settled on one of her mother walking along the beach with three small girls in tow.

"I got it!" Essie spouted as she backed away and

plopped onto the sofa. "At least the contraption works. I was afraid we'd have to go to thrift stores to look for a working VCR."

Remembering her mother's letter, Hannah asked, "Where's that letter? It said something about setting the clock to five."

She moved some of the videocassettes and found their mother's letter beneath them. "Yes, here it is. 'Set the clock dial to five o'clock and give the pendulum a nudge.' Says we'll discover magic when we do. Let's give it a try and see what happens."

Hannah and her sisters looked over at the silent ancient clock that never kept good time. Its face stared back at them, silent and still.

Walking to the clock, Hannah asked, "Think it works when it's set at five o'clock? I remember it being set to five when Dad was here, and we were playing games around the kitchen table. The next morning it was back to nine-fifteen."

She opened the small glass pane covering its gold embossed face. She turned the hands so that they read the correct time. After shutting the pane, she reached down to give the pendulum a nudge.

The gold pendulum swung rhythmically and continually. A soft ticking sound filled the room, counting off the passing seconds while the three sisters looked at it in amazement.

"Wow," Essie said from in front of the TV. "I can't believe it's working."

The sound of girls laughing interrupted them. Turning around, they watched videos of themselves as children playing on the beach in front of the little cottage. They worked together to build a sand castle that looked impressive to them. Giggles and squeals of delight came from the TV as the three women saw themselves as they used to be. Young. Happy. Sisters.

The images mesmerized Hannah, taking her back to days when life was much simpler. Without taking her eyes off the TV, she found her way back to her place in the chair and folded her legs. Her mind wandered into the past as shown on the TV.

The scene was something out of a childhood dream, yet she remembered the day vividly. It was one of the few days her father came home to visit. He must have taken the video of them.

Playing in the sand with her sisters seemed like the best thing in life back then. Her mother was sitting in a shaded chair. The ocean reached for them, and pulled back out while big fluffy clouds wandered around the sky.

Her father. Where was he? Probably still traveling like he'd been all her life. In and out on rare occasions. Never staying for long. He'd been a father in name only since little bonding had taken place between them.

He might be the reason her sisters disliked each other so much now. None of them had had the influence of a father in their lives.

She stirred herself out of her daydream and focused on the TV. The scene was the beach, with a young Hannah who was barely walking. Her older sisters held her hands as they walked across the wet sand, followed by their mother as she watched to make sure they stayed out of the reach of the waves coming ashore. The toddler stumbled, but the strong hands of her sisters kept her from falling. When toddler Hannah stopped to reach for a seashell, they bent down to look at it together.

Hannah's eyes stung as she watched the care the older sisters had with her. The smiles and laughter spoke volumes about the love and happiness of that day long ago. Her heart softened slightly.

Essie pointed the remote at the VCR and pushed a button. "It won't fast forward," she cried out, repeatedly pushing the button. "It won't work!"

Sharon took the remote from Essie. "You don't know how to work it right. Let me do it." She pushed the button repeatedly, but with the same result.

Hannah rubbed her eyes and said, "Mother did this on purpose." Her voice crackled a little and she cleared her throat. Her mother's purpose was finally clear, and she didn't necessarily like it. "She's trying to get us to play nice together."

Sharon sniffed. "I think you're right. It hurt her feelings we no longer spoke to each other. She thought she could show us how things used to be, and we'd make amends."

Essie got up and started for her bedroom. "I refuse to be manipulated by someone from the grave." She stomped off down the hallway and slammed her door.

Sharon chuckled softly as she sat on the sofa beside Hannah. "She's been the stubbornest of us three, don't you think?" Sharon looked at Hannah with expectant eyes.

Hannah agreed. "And the bossiest. Being the oldest, she always thought she was in charge when Mother wasn't around."

Sharon put her feet on the coffee table. "Do you

think Mother deliberately broke the fast forward button? Is Essie right? Is she trying to manipulate us?" Sharon's forehead wrinkled with thought.

Hannah shrugged. She didn't want to speak badly of her mother, especially not now. She might feel the same way if her sons didn't get along with each other. She might resort to the same tricks her mother was using. In fact, it was a pretty good idea.

Inwardly, she smiled. Maybe she'd use the same strategy someday if her sons became estranged from each other.

She looked at the clock to see how long they'd been watching the videos. The clock still read five o'clock as it still ticked off seconds loudly. She dismissed the notion of a working clock with a shrug and an eye roll. Even when it went tick-tock, it didn't keep the right time. Nothing was magical about the broken clock, other than it was ticking.

They should call a repairman and see if something could be done to make it run right.

Chapter 8

Essie

Essie lay on the twin bed in her room that still had her old pink bedspread on it. Nothing had changed since she left for college long ago. In the corner, a shelf held stuffed animals that were likely collectibles now. Even her old Star Wars posters were still tacked on the wall.

She cocked her head a little so she could see them more clearly. Her children loved the same Star Wars movies. They would love the posters and might even fight over them. They were in pristine condition. She could sell them for a little extra money. If she could find someone to pay a nice sum for the original posters, she'd get her new stove after all. She got up and started to take them down.

Moving to her closet, she found her old Nancy Drew and Hardy Boys books. She loved reading those mystery books when she was younger. Her children would likely love them too. She took the books down and scattered them on her bed. Those must come home with her.

The sounds of her rambunctious children at

home filled her mind and her heart. They were on the other side of the planet, but she could imagine their playful banter. She hung on to the mental sounds while she hung her clothes up.

She rolled up the posters before stacking the books on the dresser top. Looking around, the sounds of her children left her mind, and the room seemed bare and empty.

She didn't like quiet. She needed her children's noises to be happy. The ache to go home filled her heart, making her clutch her chest. It was her happy place.

Hannah was right. They needed to get this done quickly, and if that meant staying up all night, she'd do it. But first, she needed a box to pack her childhood treasures in.

As Essie left her room, she could hear the VCR machine playing. Glancing at the TV screen as she walked by the sofa, she saw her sisters pushing her in a wagon to the edge of a hill. The wagon went a few feet before gravity pulled it the rest of the way down the grassy hill. At the bottom, she jumped out and pulled the wagon back to the top for another sister to take her turn to ride down.

"I remember that hill," Essie said as she sat down on the sofa. "We would go by there on our way to the market. Mother would let us play on the hill for a little while before we got groceries and pulled them home in the wagon." She laughed as the video showed the wagon full of little girls rolling down the hill. Her sisters' laughter blended with her own.

Realizing she was enjoying the video, she stopped laughing and stood. "I don't have time for this.

My family needs me to get home as soon as I can. Why can't we fast forward over this?"

Her sisters didn't look away from the TV screen to look at her. Hannah said in a monotone voice, "Mother must have sabotaged it. She didn't want us to rush over the memories."

Essie let out a loud sputter, mad at her Mother for forcing this on her. "Why don't we go buy one that does? It would speed up the process. Let's find the last tape so we can go home! I refuse to let Mom brainwash me or manipulate me into doing something I don't want to do."

Sharon turned sideways on the couch to look at Essie. "What're you afraid of? Afraid you might find something about us to like? Afraid you might see you had a happy childhood?"

Essie put a hand on her hip. "I'm not afraid of anything of the sort! I'll make up my own mind on how I feel about you. I heard you two calling me bossy. Someone must take charge, or we'll be here until Gabriel sounds his horn. Plus, I'm thinking of my children and how they need me at home. Now, if you don't mind, I need to find boxes to pack some things I want to take with me."

Hannah jumped up from her seat. "Wait a minute! What are you taking?"

"Stuff out of *my* room! *My* posters and *my* books."

"Your books!" Hannah shrieked as she started around the sofa to get into Essie's personal space. "I promised my son I'd bring books home for him. I want a chance to go through those books too."

"They're mine!" Essie yelled, getting into

Hannah's face. "Mom bought those books for me. That's why they're in my room."

Sharon made several tries to get out of the overstuffed, oversoft sofa. Finally succeeding, she joined in the showdown. "We haven't talked about how we're going to split stuff in the house yet. Don't go running off with the good stuff. I might want those Star Wars posters."

Essie had her fists clenched more from stress than a physical threat. Her sisters had their hands on their hips in defiance of her suggestion at taking things from her room. Neither seemed willing to let her do what she wanted with her stuff. It was time to stake her territory.

The three sisters faced off while around them drifted the sound of their young-girl laughter.

An angry scream, followed by childish crying, projected from the TV. All three women heard their mother's gentle yet firm voice say, "Girls, play nice! You have to share."

Essie felt the atmosphere in the room change. She unclenched her fists and watched as her sisters' faces turned incredulous, letting go of the anger that only a second before threatened to burst into an all-out fight.

All three turned to look at the TV screen where their mother was leaning over her daughters, making them hug each other in forgiveness.

Essie's throat started hurting with the lump forming there. She held up her hands in surrender. "Fine. Let's each go through our rooms and share what we'd like to take out of them. We can surely come to an agreement on how to divide Mom's stuff."

Sharon took a step back. "Sounds like a good plan to me. What do you say, Hannah?"

Hannah didn't speak, but nodded before returning to her seat in the overstuffed chair.

Essie's stomach roiled in emotional discomfort. Too much stress. She needed to get away. She needed time to think things through.

She glanced at the grandfather clock and saw it still read five o'clock. "Still five, huh. Mother left us a broken clock. I'll let you two fight over it."

She yelled out over her shoulder as she walked toward the front door. "Anyone object to me going down to the beach for little while? I need a walk to calm down."

Hannah didn't look up, but kept her arms folded across her chest and her eyes on the video. "Good idea." The frown on her face made it clear she didn't want to hear anything else.

Essie went to the back door in the kitchen. She pulled on the door knob, but it didn't budge. She made sure the deadbolt was pulled back and tugging harder, she pulled on the door knob again. Nothing. She walked into the living room and tried that door. It was as firmly stuck as the back door.

"What's up?" Sharon asked as she watched Essie trying the door. "I thought you were going for a walk."

Essie tugged on the door. "I can't get either door to open. I thought the back door was swelled shut because of the humidity. I tried this one and it seems the same. We didn't have any trouble coming in. I wonder why I can't get out?" She tried the door again.

With a sigh like a teenager asked to do a chore, Hannah got up and tried to open the door. It still refused to budge. She tried again, but got the same result.

Essie scratched her head. Something strange was going on. "Let's both pull on it," she told Hannah.

She put her hands around the door knob and Hannah put her hands on top. Together they pulled and the door moved slightly.

Backing off to regather strength, they tried again. Hannah put her foot on the casing for leverage. Giving it a mighty pull, the sound of a vacuum unsealing echoed around the room.

The clock gave a mighty gong and went silent as the door flung open, sending them both backward. Essie tripped over the edge of the rug and fell on the tile floor.

Hannah tripped over Essie and landed with a hard thud beside her.

Sharon rushed over and helped Hannah stand. "What's going on here? What was that sucking noise I heard when the door opened? And that clock! I've never heard it chime. That was weird!" She reached out a hand to help Essie up.

Essie lay on the floor trying to get her senses back in order. When her head quit spinning, she found nothing hurt other than her backside. She sat on the floor. "It's like we were sealed in here. Listen."

The three women stopped moving.

Sharon turned to look at the TV. "The video has gone off."

"And the clock is not ticking," Hannah said in a shaky voice as she rubbed her hip. "It says nine fifteen again. It still read five o'clock when I looked at it a few minutes ago."

Essie got up off the floor and led her sisters over to the clock. "Now it says nine fifteen, like when we got here and it wasn't working. There's something strange about that clock."

A shudder ran through Essie that the others must have felt because they seemed to shudder too. "What's the real time?" she asked them.

Hannah pulled her cell phone from her pocket. "Says it's two thirty. But how can that be? We started watching these videos about then and we've been watching for at least a couple of hours."

Sharon went to her purse and pulled out her cell phone. "Mine says two thirty-one. I don't get it. It should be supper time. This is freaking me out!" She started her panic-panting and Essie helped her to her place on the sofa.

"Wait a minute!" Hannah said. "Something must be wrong with the cell phone service. Let me call my house—it's the same time zone as here—and find out what time it really is. Besides, I need to check to make sure Horace talked to Mrs. Hagg about getting the clothes to the dry cleaners."

She hit redial and put the phone on speaker. Soon they heard Horace's voice on the phone. "Horace," Hannah said with a sweet falsetto in her voice, "Oh, good, you're still there. What time is it? I know it's a dumb question, but what time is it?"

"Two-thirty-two. Why?"

Hannah's face paled as she turned to look at her sisters. She spoke softly into the phone again. "What time did I call to tell you about getting your dad's clothes to the dry cleaners?"

"It was like five minutes ago."

Essie felt light-headed as she watched the color drain from Hannah's face and her eyes widen. Sharon stood with her hand over her mouth, her eyes wide with fright.

Essie's mind couldn't fathom what was going on. The world was disoriented, and she along with it.

Hannah stuttered. "Are—are you sure it was only five minutes ago? I—I thought I called two hours ago."

Silence filled the room until Horace asked, "Mom, are you all right? You called me a few minutes ago. Are you like having a stroke or something?"

The sisters turned to look at the now-silent clock, sitting beside the fireplace with its secrets intact. Its eerie stillness sent shivers down their spines.

Hannah held the phone against her stomach as she took a deep breath. Her phone shook slightly as she replied, "No, I'm fine. I guess I lost track of time. Thanks, honey. Don't forget to talk to Mrs. Hagg." She hung up and dropped her phone on the chair.

Sharon put her hand over her heart. "I think I'll find a hotel room in town."

"No, no, no!" Essie said, shaking her head and wagging her finger. "No one is leaving here until we figure this out. We'll stay here until we find the one video Mother wants us to see."

Essie walked over to the clock and gave it close examination. She was either losing her mind or maybe—just maybe—their Mother had truly left them a magical gift. "Mother said it was a magical clock. I guess we've discovered its magic. It alters time."

Hannah came up behind her. "It alters time? That's crazy! That's science fiction talk. Nothing can alter time."

Essie put her face close to the old clock's dial. Nothing unusual stood out other than its age. Its design was reflective of a long-ago era, like something found in a museum. She ran her hands over the smooth wood, but didn't find any hidden compartments or unusual cavities.

Looking at its face again, she saw a tiny little lever that she pushed which allowed the face to open. Pulling the door open, she could see a few unmoving gold cogs, but nothing else. The clock workings looked ordinary enough to her untrained eyes.

She closed the door and stood back. "Looks like a normal clock, but there's something odd about it. It doesn't work unless it's set to five o'clock. Makes no sense."

Essie mumbled to herself as she made her way back to the sofa. "Let's think about this. It's never kept good time and now we know why. It makes time stand still. It's magic like Mom said. What's strange about magic?"

She looked at her sisters who looked as mystified as she felt.

Hannah returned to her seat. "We deal in magic all the time. Most people don't believe we exist. And we do! A magic clock shouldn't be staggering to our imaginations."

Sharon joined Essie on the sofa. "You're right. But where would Mother get a clock like that? And why didn't she tell us about it before now?"

Essie shrugged. "Who knows. Maybe she got it from her mother. Or her grandmother."

"The answer may be on the videos." Sharon

grabbed the remotes from the top of the coffee table. "I hope the machine didn't die when we opened the door." Pushing the power button, the machines whirred to life, and the video started showing again.

Essie settled back, wiggling her backside down deep into the sofa. "Let's not set the clock for a little bit and check our cell phone times again. Just to make sure our theory is right."

She watched her cell phone count off the minutes as the video showed its recorded images. Certain that the clock was the magician, she turned the video off.

Rubbing her temples, she said, "Mother obviously wanted us to watch the videos while time stood still so we could watch them all. We wouldn't spend much time away from our families if time stood still while we're watching. It's considerate of her, yet still manipulative."

"But why?" Hannah stretched her legs out in front of her. "Why not leave one video telling us what she wanted from us? Why make us watch them all?"

"That's obvious," Sharon noted. "She wants us to see how we used to be and hopes we'll make peace between us. She wants us to be sisters again."

Releasing a sound that was a cross between a roar and a groan of frustration, Essie said, "That conniving woman! She's trying to manipulate us into liking each other. Like that's going to happen."

When her sisters didn't follow along with the complaining, she realized she was being unreasonable. It wasn't good to speak evil of the dead, especially her mother. "You're right, Sharon. Sounds like something she'd do."

Hannah frowned. "It hurt her that we didn't like each other. She said that the last time I talked to her."

Essie knew Hannah was right. Again. Her mother had told her the same thing. Guilt for hurting her mother washed over Essie like a bucket of cold water poured over her head.

She remembered her resolution from this morning, to be more diplomatic and tactful. She'd failed miserably. Being the oldest, it was up to her to set the example and try harder to get along with her sisters. If her mother was watching over them, it would please her to see them trying to get along.

Hannah added in her unemotional manner. "It's too late to change things. All we can do is live with regret."

Sharon quickly sat up straight on the sofa. "No! It's not too late!"

Surprised at Sharon's outburst, Essie said, "So where do we go from here? Does it matter what Mom wants us to do or do we choose our own course of action?"

The trio exchanged looks. Sharon had tears in her eyes. Essie knew how she would vote. Hannah's tone of voice indicated she didn't care as long as it didn't keep her here too long. Essie knew she had the deciding vote.

The image of her mother sitting in this cottage alone every day popped into her head and pushed her emotions to decide the matter. She was the oldest. And bossiest according to her sisters. She'd keep them on track.

Standing taller, Essie told her sisters, "She wanted us to come together and watch these videos.

Out of respect for her wishes, let's do what she wanted. Let's renew our truce."

She paused long enough to get concurrence. Her sisters nodded.

Continuing, she added, "We can go back to hating each other after we go home. If time stands still while we look for the right video, we won't be late getting back home. And we'll have granted our mother's wish."

Hannah shrugged. "As long as I'm home by Halloween, I don't care. Remember we're stuck in here while the clock is working or slowing time or whatever it's doing."

Essie watched Hannah shuffle off to her room as the sound of girlish laughter and shouts filled the living room again.

Sharon went toward the clock, but stopped at the same time Essie heard the sound. Was that knocking at the door real or on the video?

Chapter 9

Sharon

Sharon's hand froze in front of the clock as a second hard knock on the door echoed around the room. She turned to see Essie looking as puzzled as she felt.

Hannah came back in the room and asked, "Was that a knock I heard?"

Essie and Hannah went to the door. Sharon followed close behind them, but kept them between her and whatever was causing such a racket on the front porch.

Essie opened the door. The afternoon sun shone in brightly across the beach, silhouetting the imposing figure standing there.

Sharon took a step away from the intimidating figure.

A slightly familiar, booming voice came into the room ahead of the man. "Hello, ladies!" The large man took a step forward, and the light from the front window lit his face.

Sharon breathed a sigh of relief when she recognized Mr. Howard in the front entrance.

He stomped his feet on the rug at the door sill. "I was passing by and wanted to make sure you had everything you need."

Hannah had a frown in her voice. "We live at the end of a dead-end street. How could you be passing by?"

The man laughed heartily. "You caught me in a lie. I came out here on purpose to make sure everything was as you expected it to be. Do you have groceries? I brought you milk and eggs. Everybody needs those! I could go get more groceries if you give me a list."

Essie replied, making no move to take the offered sack. "We have enough food for several days."

Mr. Howard did a little dance of impatience in the doorway. "I thought I'd reiterate my offer. When you decide to sell this place, I'll make you a great offer. I've been looking for a place like this to get away from the city and relax." He craned his neck to see around the corner into the kitchen. "Looks very charming."

Sharon stepped around Essie and stood beside Hannah, blocking his view from the rest of the cottage. "It's not for sale."

Essie pushed the door. It bumped Mr. Howard to indicate the visit was over. He refused to budge and took a step past the door. He looked at his feet, as if looking for where to step to get around the ladies.

They stood firm against him.

Relenting, he said, "Okay, I wanted you to know. I hope you'll call me if you needed anything." He held the sack of milk and eggs out again.

This time, Essie took it and handed it to Sharon.

He tapped his fingertips together as if looking for an excuse to stay. After long uncomfortable silence passed, a look of resignation passed across his face when no invitation came. "I guess I should go." He paused, ostensibly giving them one last chance to invite him in. Getting no offer, he bid them good-bye.

While Essie shut the door and locked it, Sharon took the sack to the kitchen to put things away. Her attention was drawn to the window facing the driveway. She watched as Mr. Howard left the sidewalk to look around the outside of the house and in the yard.

She waved her sisters into the kitchen, to the window so they could watch him. Her words were hard to speak because of the anger she felt. "Look at him! Who does he think he is? We told him no! I wish I had a few of our guard reindeer here to sic on him, the nosy old coot. They would make short work of getting this unwanted visitor off the property."

Hannah let out a snarl. "I'm going to get rid of him." She started for the door, but her sisters held her back.

Together, they watched him look behind the house and step off the length of the yard. After a few minutes, he got into his expensive car and drove away.

"He's going to be a problem," Hannah said with an icy tone. "I think I'll call Headless and see if he won't pay him a visit one night. If he thought this place was haunted, he'd leave us alone."

Horrified at the thought of a headless man visiting the overweight lawyer, Sharon choked out, "He might have a heart attack with a visit from Headless. I can talk to Santa and Elwin. They could send the guard reindeer that won't let anyone around here. They'd chase him out of the yard in short order. Although it's a little too hot for reindeer around here. They wouldn't like it too much."

"I'd like to pelt him and his car with eggs," Essie added as they watched the car get smaller in the distance. She tapped her chin with her finger. "I wonder what would have happened if he'd come while the clock was set to five. Do you think he could have told that we were messing with time in here?"

A bolt of fear shot through Sharon like lightning, causing her breath to speed up. They hadn't considered anyone outside of the house feeling the impacts. "It may not be a good idea to mess with time. Do you think Mr. Howard knew we were messing with it? Could he sense something like that?"

Her heart raced with her imaginations growing larger and more frightening. "Do you think the government can tell we are messing with the natural flow of time? What if we changed the course of history without knowing it? Maybe we shouldn't use the clock at all. It's too dangerous!"

She stumbled toward the sofa, holding her head that was spinning with its visions of police raiding their peaceful little cottage.

Essie helped her back to the sofa. "You still have those anxiety attacks?"

Sharon nodded while holding her tightening chest.

Essie sat on the coffee table facing Sharon. "Calm down, everything will be fine. Remember what Mother used to say. Breathe slowly." She held Sharon's face and breathed slowly.

Seeing Essie's breathing rhythm helped her slow her own. Sharon held her breath for a few seconds and let out a long sigh. She followed Essie's lead, and the two of them breathed slowly until Sharon's head cleared.

Hannah looked at the two of them with a bored expression. "How could anyone know about the clock? The government would have snatched it years ago if they'd known Mother used it. She didn't get in trouble. Neither will we."

Sharon's imagination was starting to run away with her again. "Did she use it? How do we know?"

Maybe her mother had never used it. But how would she know to tell them what time to set it to so they would watch videos without time passing? She swayed as her head started spinning again.

Essie grabbed her face and made her breathe slowly along with her.

After she got her breathing under control, Sharon leaned back and made her muscles relax. She put her feet on the table beside Essie, and hoped it didn't break under the weight of her feet and Essie. Out of the corner of her eye, she could see the disapproving frown on Hannah's face.

Essie tapped her chin with her finger again and said, "Why don't we run a little experiment?" She eyed the other sisters. "What if one of us goes outside while the other two stay in here to set the clock? The ones inside will run the video machine for one hour. We'll stop the clock and find out what happened outside."

Sharon froze. Messing with time seemed wrong. Like tempting fate or something. "One of us go outside? But what if we can't get back in? Or we end up in different times?" Her breath quickened.

Waving her hands downward to calm Sharon,

Essie said, "Take a deep breath, Sharon. The lawyer's visit proved once we stop the clock, things go back to being an ordinary cottage. There's nothing to be afraid of."

Sharon still wasn't sure. Everything was happening too fast. Finding out her mother was gone. Getting a cottage with a strange clock. Being with her sisters who were strangers to her. She thought of Santa and the elves back home, snug in their stone condos and workshop. She yearned to be there with them.

Hannah let out a loud cry, pulling Sharon out of her wishful thinking. "Great idea! I'll be the one who goes outside. It'll be dark soon, my favorite time of day, and I need a break. You two stay here and run the videos for an hour. Let's see what happens."

Relieved not to be the guinea pig stuck outside, Sharon's heart slowed slightly. "We'll watch half of a video. That's about an hour."

Essie stood up, a video in her hand. "Sounds like a plan. Sharon, you get ready to set the grandfather clock and Hannah, we'll see you in an hour."

Sharon went to the grandfather clock and got ready to set the dial to five o'clock. She moved the hands to the correct time.

Hannah took her station outside, stretching her arms to take in the view.

Essie shut the door and signaled for Sharon to start the grandfather clock while she started the new video.

Sharon gave the pendulum a nudge. The experiment began.

Chapter 10

Hannah

Hannah stood on the steps of the porch and took a deep breath. The fresh sea air felt good in her lungs. The beach called to her, and she was ready to answer.

The overwhelming urge to walk on the beach pushed her forward. She took one step off the porch when the door opened behind her. Swinging around, she saw her sisters in the doorway.

She didn't understand. Why hadn't they started the clock yet? "I'm ready to start the experiment when you are." She pointed over her shoulder to the beach. Why were her sisters holding her back?

Essie's eyes widened. "It's over. We've been watching the video for an hour."

A tiny shiver went up Hannah's spine. "Are you sure? I took one step and here you are." All she'd done was take a breath. An hour inside. A second outside. Time seemed malleable.

A tremor spread across Sharon's body. "That clock is creepy!"

Hannah laughed. "It's not creepy. It's great! We could almost live forever with a clock like that!"

Sharon cried out, "Shush, Hannah!" Looking around the porch while searching for overhearing ears and spying eyes, she shushed her sister again. "We shouldn't talk about this out here. You never know who might be watching. Or listening."

She waved Hannah back into the house. "I have a strange feeling about that Howard man. He could be spying on us."

Hannah covered her mouth and went quickly into the house. "You're right. We need to be careful talking about this around others. It's a secret best kept between the three of us." She made the motion of zipping her mouth shut.

Sharon shut the door. "Could you see if anything strange was going on inside the house?" she asked Hannah.

"No, I didn't look. I was going to go to the beach. My back was to the house."

"We have to do this again," Sharon wailed as she wrung her hands, "except this time you need to watch the house. See if lightning shoots out of the windows."

"Whhaaat?" Hannah's voice rose an octave, wondering if she'd heard right. "Lightning shoots out the windows? Doesn't happen. I think I'd have noticed that even with my back turned."

Sharon pounded her fists together in rhythm with the words. "We need to make sure we aren't drawing attention to ourselves." Having emphasized her concerns, she began wringing her hands. "We have to make sure nothing happens outside to show we are messing with time."

From the kitchen, Essie called out, "I don't think

we need to repeat the test." She came out of the kitchen with a cookie in her hand.

"This is important!" Sharon's voice grew loud and panicky. She looked at her sisters for support. "What if someone finds out we can alter time? What happens if, and after we go home, someone breaks in to steal the clock because they know what it will do?"

Hannah dropped her head to her chest. There was no reasoning with Sharon. She bit her tongue to keep the words back she wanted to say to her over-worried, over-weight, over-sensitive sister. They had an agreement to get along, and she would honor it.

She started toward the front door. "Fine!" The words came out like a snakebite, fast and venomous. She paused to let the anger bubbling close to the surface simmer down a little. "If it makes you feel better, we'll do this experiment again."

Essie sat on the sofa and rubbed her temples. "We'll crack the curtains a little. Hannah, see what shows out there. Lightning. Sky turning orange. A light from heaven. Whatever."

Letting out a loud sigh, Hannah opened the door. "This seems silly to me. Mother used the clock, and no one bothered her about it. When we use the clock, all we have to do is shut the curtains and make sure they are completely closed."

Sharon waved her hands wildly. "Doesn't it bother either of you what this might look like to others if they saw it? What if Mr. Howard looked in before he knocked at the door and saw we were moving at the speed of light or whatever it looks like in here. He'd think it was odd and report us to someone and they'd come to investigate. The government might come take the clock away! We have to be sure about this!"

This silly talk was giving Hannah a headache. She grimaced as she pinched the bridge of her nose. "Calm down! I said we'd do it again." Opening the door, she stepped in the doorway. "This time, wait for me to turn around and look at the house."

Sharon let out a victorious cry as she ran to the clock.

Her beaming smile made Hannah give Essie a roll of her eyes, which was returned. Hannah walked outside into the front porch.

Surveying the picture window facing the beach, Hannah told Essie, "Draw the curtains. I'll check for any cracks between them to see if anything shines through."

Essie adjusted the curtains, leaving a few places to see through. When everything was set right, Essie shut the door to conduct their next experiment.

Hannah took her place outside the window and signaled to begin the process. Looking through the slit in the curtain, she could see nothing but blackness. It was like trying to see in a window on a bright sunny day.

Just as before, she waited for only a few seconds before the front door opened and her sisters waved her back inside.

Essie greeted her first as she came inside. "We watched a whole video before coming out, to make sure our theory is correct."

Sharon looked anxious. "What did you see? Anything that would suggest something suspicious going on inside?"

Hannah shook her head. "I saw nothing. It was

too dark to see anything inside, and no lightning shot out the window. The sky stayed blue, and the waves went in and out just like normal. Sharon, you have nothing to worry about." She gave her sister a smirk and got a bright grin in return.

Essie sat in the overstuffed chair and snuggled into it. "How did time feel out there?"

"It felt like thirty seconds. Wow, hard to imagine we can control time like that by moving the hands on an old clock." They turned to look at the silent timepiece. The clock that never worked actually did. It altered time.

A strange sound faintly rumbled. Sharon grabbed her stomach. "Sorry. I guess I'm hungry. When was the last time we ate?"

"Who knows?" Hannah said as she took her place in the overstuffed chair. "I can't put a number on the time any more. I'm not sure what day it is."

"Whatever time it is, I'm hungry too." Essie got up and headed into the kitchen.

Hannah couldn't remember when she ate last. How many hours had it been? Depended on how she looked at it.

She got up and followed her sisters into the kitchen. "Hey girls, this is going to mess up my sleep patterns."

Later that night—or whatever time it was outside the cottage—Hannah lay on the comfortable sofa in the dark living room in her leggings and t-shirt, listening to the ticking clock and watching the TV. Her cell phone said it was two o'clock in the morning, but it had said the same time for hours.

She rummaged through the large bowl of popcorn in her lap while she watched another video. The stack of videos on the kitchen table was growing as she and her sisters took turns watching them. The closet still held more than she dared to count.

Sometimes Hannah enjoyed seeing scenes from her childhood. Many things she'd forgotten or hadn't thought of in a long time were there on the TV. The flood of emotions and remembrances of simpler times would occasionally moisten her eyes and make her nose run.

Scenes from her happy childhood would pull her in and she'd forget about what she was supposed to be doing, looking for their mother's last wishes. A little pang of guilt would nick her heart, making her heart bleed tears. She should have come home more often for the sake of her mother. It would have made her happy.

She thought of her sons. She was closer to Horace because he was the oldest and first to communicate with her. Huntley was so much like his father that he seemed to be closer to Headless than her. Regardless of that, she loved them both more than she'd thought possible. Being their mother was one of the best things that had ever happened to her.

Watching the videos, she saw the care and kindness her mother had shown to her daughters. She watched over them carefully when they were in the water. She took care of their scrapes and bruises. She comforted them when they cried. Never was there a hint of anything but love in her actions.

A lump in her throat expanded so much it hurt and forced more tears to flow. The videos showed the truth. Her mother loved her girls as much as she loved her sons. She sniffled and blew her nose into a tissue.

Sharon's voice came softly through the darkness. "They're affecting you like they do me." She came around the edge of the sofa, dressed in her long red nightgown.

The sound startled Hannah, but didn't scare her. Sitting up on the sofa, she quickly dried her eyes and cleared her throat of the fading lump. She put the bowl of popcorn in the middle of the sofa. "I'd forgotten so much. Brings back memories and makes me nostalgic. She was a great mother to us."

Sharon sat down at the other end of the sofa and took a few kernels of popcorn. "I'd forgotten too. I cried a lot during my last shift." She took a handful of popcorn and began munching on it.

Hannah wished Sharon would go back to bed. She wanted to be left alone with her emotions and feel free to cry if she felt like it. "What are you doing up this time of night?"

Sharon stared at the screen. "I awoke and couldn't go back to sleep. I understand why Mother had us do this exercise. She wanted to remind of us of how it used to be and how we used to be a family."

Hannah snuggled deeper into the corner of the soft leather sofa. "I know. But I'm like Essie, I still feel manipulated."

"I don't think she meant it. I think she's making one last-ditch effort to help us get over the hurts that have kept us apart."

Hannah heaved a sigh, hoping Sharon would take the hint. She didn't want to discuss this right now. This was her shift and she wanted to be left in peace. She should come right out and say it. She drew in a breath to speak, but was interrupted by Sharon.

"I'm sorry, Hannah, for ruining your wedding day. You were right to feel hurt by our insensitive remarks about your black wedding dress. I'm sorry for how I treated you and Headless and the things I said. I should have been more understanding." Her voice broke a little. "I'm sorry." She grabbed a handful of popcorn and stuffed it into her mouth.

Hannah sat stunned. No one had ever apologized to her for that day. Or any of the other days. Her sisters had never approved of her choices in dress, friends, or spouse. She felt like she was an outsider, distanced from their highly-respected spouses and their highly-respected holidays. She and Headless were always on the outer fringes. She wasn't sure she was ready to forgive yet.

Hannah sat up a little. "The videos brought all that on?" In the light of the TV, she saw Sharon nod.

Playing with the hem of her nightgown, Sharon spoke softly, "I've been wrapped up in my life and my work I forgot about my first family. I have my own family now, and I've forgotten the family I started from. You, me, Essie, Mother, Grandmother. And Father." Sharon looked over at Hannah. "You remember much about Father?"

A vague image floated through her mind. Everyone had told her she looked like him. "I don't remember a lot. He wandered in and out and never stayed for long."

Essie came walking into the living room in her lilac flannel nightgown. "I probably remember a little more since I'm older." She settled into the overstuffed chair. "When we were younger, he came in summer.

When we were older, he came in fall. He never came any other times. Mother said he came when his appearance matched her age and ours. There was less to explain to neighbors if he looked like he belonged."

Hannah picked up the mostly empty bowl of popcorn and slid it across the coffee table toward Essie.

Her memories of her father were faint and she'd wondered about him. Her older sisters remembered things she didn't. As long as she was forfeiting her quiet time, the topic of their father was a good trade.

Chapter 11

Essie

Essie snuggled deeper into the overstuffed chair chair and pulled her cool feet under her gown. The humidity seeped through the flannel gown, chilling her bones. The moist night air left her chilly though the temperature was warm by most standards. She curled up and waited for her body heat to warm the chair.

Sharon continued the conversation. "I remember Father a little. He flitted in and out of our lives. We usually saw him once a year as I remember, for a couple of weeks or a month. I don't feel like I ever got to know him."

Essie agreed. "Mother told everyone he had a high-powered international job keeping him on the road all the time. I asked her what he did in his job and she said it was complicated. 'He keeps the universe in sync,' she said. Whatever that means. I still have no idea what he does exactly."

She hadn't thought of her father in a long time. Tall, lean, and handsome, she understood why her mother was taken with him. She must have really loved him, to be left with raising three girls mostly on her own.

Putting her feet on the coffee table, Sharon leaned back. "Do you think when they sent us outside to play, that they set the clock to five so they could have more time together?" The question hung in the air like clothes hanging on a line, whipped by the breeze of imagination.

"Weird." Hannah chomped on more popcorn. "Not sure I want to think about it."

Essie stared at her sister. Weird? Who was she calling weird? And this coming from a goth who was married to a headless guy who loved horses. What was her definition of weird?

Essie shook her head. She needed to clear her mind of its weirdness.

Sharon stood up. "Shall I make hot cocoa?" Hearing no objections, she went to the kitchen.

Essie and Hannah stared at the TV, watching a Christmas scene. The tree looked small behind the mound of gifts under and around it. It was the Christmas of the bicycles. All three girls got new bikes whose parts and pieces were wrapped individually, making it look like a bounty of gifts.

Their mother and grandmother took the time to take the bikes apart and wrapped the parts separately. Together, they put the bikes back together, and in doing so, they taught the girls how to do it too. After that, their mother left the maintenance needs up to the girls.

"I still have my bike from that Christmas," Hannah said in a voice sounding more like she was talking to herself. "It's hanging in our garage. The boys are too proud to ride Mom's old bike, and I'm too big for it, but somehow I could never seem to let go of it."

Essie chuckled softly. "My kids used mine for spare parts. It's still around, spread out in different places. I taught them how to keep their bikes in good working order."

Sharon brought in three mugs of hot cocoa, filling the living room with the delicious chocolate aroma. "I got rid of my bike a long time ago. Not many chances to use it where I live. The reindeer take us wherever we need to go."

The warm delicious liquid warmed Essie as it went down. She felt cozy and fuzzy inside. "I suppose you don't get outside too much, Sharon. You look pale. I wondered if you'd been ill."

"We get outside in the summers. Santa and I go on a vacation for a couple of weeks about February. Otherwise we stay inside."

"Don't you get cabin fever?"

Sharon thought for a moment. "Not really. It's *cold* outside! We're busy in our large workshop and seeing after our helpers. I guess I don't take the time to think about it."

Essie sipped her cocoa as they watched their videoed bike rides down the road by their house. Their mother clapped and danced around, enjoying the day as much as the girls enjoyed their bikes. Smiles and laughs floated around the room, joining in with the ones emitting from the TV.

Setting her empty mug on the coffee table, Essie remarked, "Who's taking this video? There's us and Mother. Do either of you remember who else was there with us?"

The other two shook their heads without taking their eyes off the screen.

She settled back in. "Must have been Father or Grandmother. No one else ever came around."

Sharon put her empty mug down. "Couldn't have been Father. I don't remember him ever being around for any of the holidays other than Fourth of July, Labor Day, and a Halloween or two. Must have been Grandmother, but I don't remember—" she looked off into space for a moment, "—I don't remember her being there that summer. Do you?"

Hannah shook her head. "Does it matter? We were so caught up in our new bikes we don't remember her there. It doesn't matter. Obviously, someone was there videoing. How else would we be watching this?"

Even in the dark, Essie could almost hear her eyes roll. She nestled farther into the chair. "Had to have been her. Who else could it have been? But do you know what else is weird?"

She stopped at the sound of that word. Hannah might not think it was weird, but she did. "I don't remember being filmed this much. What year did Mother get that video camera? Were they even invented back then?"

Hannah laughed and for a flash, Essie thought it was at her use of the word weird.

Waving her hand at the TV, Hannah said, "I'm not even sure what year this is. Someone was obviously there."

Sharon sat up straighter. "Grandmother was around occasionally. We probably forgot when she was there. She and Mother looked alike. Our memories are mixed up."

Essie pointed her finger toward her sister. "You know what, Sharon? You're right! I'm sure we're getting things mixed up between Mother and Grandmother."

Sharon let out a yawn. "I think cocoa was just the thing I needed. I'm going back to bed. I can sleep now. Good night!" She struggled out of her cozy spot on the sofa and went down the hallway to her room.

Essie stared at Hannah. "Why don't you go to bed too. I'm not sleepy anymore. I can take over watching."

Hannah stretched her long legs and yawned. "I think I'll take you up on that offer. That cocoa made me sleepy too. Good night—or whatever it is." Yawning again, she rose and went to her room.

A soft click of the door let Essie know she was finally alone. She moved to the sofa, bringing an afghan with her, and stretched out the length of it. She lay on her side with her head on a pillow.

The video flickered and the scene jumped to a new recording showing her in her early teens, maybe a freshman in high school. Sharon followed her everywhere, being much less outgoing than Essie. Essie tolerated Sharon's shadowing, but when it came to Hannah, who was in fourth grade at the time, there was no tolerance for the little nuisance.

On the video, teenaged Essie pushed little girl Hannah away from her. Essie paraded around in front of the camera while Sharon mirrored Essie's movements, only behind her. In the background, Hannah dug the toe of her shoe into the dirt as she looked away with a hurt look on her face.

Essie buried her face in her hands. If her older

girls treated their younger sisters that way, she'd lecture them sternly and given them extra chores to do or ground them for a month or more.

She parted her fingers to watch as her mother bent down to assuage Hannah's hurting heart with a hug and smooth her long hair. Essie's heart felt heavy after witnessing the scene. Her mother wasn't there to give her a hug or smooth her hair or to ease her heartache.

Rummaging around on the coffee table, she found the remote and hit stop. Unrecorded memories flooded back. She'd been hateful toward Hannah, especially after hitting puberty. After that milestone, she was too cool to associate with anyone she considered beneath her. Especially her youngest sister who had always been a little weird.

That word again. She got up to pace. No doubt her sister was weird—or it was kinder to think of it as unusual. She wore nothing but black. Her wedding was black. Like-a-funeral black. And the weirdest thing, she was married to a headless man.

Even after fifteen years, Essie hadn't accepted the fact her brother-in-law had no head attached to his body. She never told anyone about him. People thought she and Easter were weird, but they didn't know Hannah and Headless.

Essie pushed back the afghan and sat on the sofa, rubbing her temples as they throbbed.

It could be her fault. Maybe she'd pushed Hannah away so often she'd pushed her into becoming a Goth. She thought she could remember reading about how most of those teens were outcasts and troubled. Had her actions those years ago affected her sister that way? Was she to blame for how her sister's life had turned out?

Unable to remain still, she got up to pace across the cool floor in her bare feet as she thought about her children. They were a close family, weren't they? She hoped so. Following her mother's example, she had lots of picnics, special dinners, and special projects around the house for the holidays. Those activities followed her philosophy that the family who plays together stays together. Was it enough?

All seven of her girls seemed to get along with each other, but did they really? On occasion, they'd argue and yell at each other, mostly over bathroom time. Other than that, they seemed to get along well, but how did they treat each other behind closed doors or when parental eyes weren't watching?

When she got home, she'd pay more attention to their interactions. She didn't want her family to fall apart. She didn't want to be alone at home, never hearing from her children. She didn't want them to treat her like she'd treated her mother. Her heart cringed in fear.

Her cold feet brought her out of her thoughts and back to the dark living room. She shook her head and pushed away the bad thoughts. Problems and worries were magnified during the night Darkness enlarged them. They overwhelmed her. The morning light would make things seem better. But wait—

Her mind whirring, she found herself staring at the clock beside the fireplace. The pendulum swung and ticked out the seconds while the hands stayed at five o'clock. The night would never end unless she stopped the clock.

She moved the hands to read nine-fifteen and stopped the pendulum. Silence returned to the room.

Looking around, she could tell no difference. She walked to the window and pulled the curtain back. The ocean reflected the thin moonlight, calling her to come closer.

She pulled the afghan off the sofa, found her shoes, and slipped them on. Wrapping the afghan around her shoulders, she opened the door and stepped outside.

The fresh cool air revived her like a slap in the face. The gray sky to the east promised sunlight that would shrink her problems to a manageable size. She filled her lungs and headed down to the beach.

Chapter 12

Sharon

A sliver of sunlight came through the gap between the curtains and fell across Sharon's face, waking her. She held her hand up to block the brightness as she yawned. Finding her cell phone on the night stand, she saw it was almost eight in the morning, an unusually late hour for her.

She stretched and got out of bed. Walking into the living room, there was no sign of her sisters. One of them had stopped the grandfather clock. It stood silent, its pendulum motionless and its hands at nine-fifteen. Time was moving at a normal pace.

The aroma of coffee might rouse the others. She headed into the kitchen. Soon she had a warm mug in her hands as she looked in the refrigerator for something to make for breakfast.

She heard the front door open, and she hurried over to see who was coming in. Essie was shutting the door behind her.

"I thought you were asleep in bed," she said, watching Essie take off her shoes and put them in the coat closet. She turned and went back in the kitchen. "Coffee?"

Flinging an afghan over the back of the overstuff chair, Essie sang out, "Love some!" She followed Sharon into the kitchen. "I couldn't sleep so I took a walk."

Sharon poured a cup of the steaming liquid and set it in front of Essie who sat at the breakfast bar. "So early in the morning?"

Essie took a sip and let out a contented sigh. "I never went to bed after Hannah did. I had too much on my mind to sleep. The video I was watching had disturbing scenes in it, and I had to get out and think."

"Disturbing scenes?"

Essie nodded before sipping more coffee. "Do you remember Hannah following us around when we were in high school?"

"I'm not sure. Why?" Sharon raised her eyebrows and wondered where this was leading as she took the seat next to Essie.

Her sister looked haggard, like too much was weighing on her mind. She was the dominant one, and Sharon was happy to allow it. Now, with Essie's stooped shoulders and sad eyes, she felt sorry for her.

Essie ran her hands through her hair and rubbed her face like she was washing it. "I didn't treat her nicely when I was a teenager. I was trying to be 'cool' and ignored Hannah's every attempt to be like me. I pushed her aside. Seeing how I treated her disgusted me."

Sharon let the confession hang in the air. The words triggered a few memories. She understood what Essie was talking about. She remembered telling

Hannah to leave her alone, but didn't all girls do that to their little sisters? Having no girls of her own, she wasn't sure.

"I remember at one point in time she was quite a nuisance, but I don't remember being mean to her. We didn't hit her. We just ignored her."

Her sister's furrowed brow and nervous hands exposed her inner turmoil over seeing how she had treated Hannah. "You might not have hit her, but I did. The video showed me physically pushing her away. I would never let my girls get away with that, and it upset me that I did it to my sister. I wonder why Mom didn't punish me?"

Sharon mused over this admission of bullying. She wasn't as surprised by the revelation as Essie seemed to be. More than once, she'd felt the brunt of Essie's highhandedness. She fought the urge to smile at her sister's weakness, now exposed, ripe for poking to see what oozed out. Surprised at the meanness in her heart, she put her elbows on the counter and took another sip of her coffee.

"You feel guilty for how you treated her?"

Essie nodded as she rubbed the sides of her coffee mug, as if smoothing them down.

"Why don't you apologize and ask her to forgive you? Seems like the logical next step."

Hannah came in the kitchen, her hair still mussed and uncombed. "Logical step for what?" She sniffed the air and declared, "That coffee smells good!"

Essie jumped like she'd received a shock from her chair. With a scowl, she told Hannah, "Don't scare me like that!"

Raising her eyebrows, Hannah held her hands

out to show she had no weapons. "What did I say?"

Sharon looked away. She'd let Essie do what she needed to do.

The silence in the kitchen filled with confusion. It made Sharon so uncomfortable that she had to say something. "Watching the videos has dredged up guilty feelings. We sometimes treated each other badly when we were growing up."

Hannah poured herself a mug of coffee and leaned against the counter. "Being the youngest, I doubt I did much of the 'treating badly' stuff. I remember being snubbed and pushed around a few times, but I thought sisters always hated each other. Seems like I read something about that somewhere. Something about competition among females for the attention of others." Unruffled, she went to the refrigerator. "What's for breakfast?"

Sharon nudged Essie. *Apologize,* she mouthed to Essie while she pointed at Hannah's back as she rummaged through the refrigerator.

Essie frowned and shook her head.

Frustrated with Essie's lack of willingness to set things right, Sharon took a bolder approach. "Hannah, Essie has something to say to you." Unfazed by Essie's glare, she waved her hand to elicit Essie's statement.

Red-faced and tight-lipped, Essie drew a ragged breath. She looked down at her hands, squeezed together so tightly her knuckles turned white.

Without looking at Hannah, she rattled off, "I'msorryItreatedyouthewayIdidwhenIwasateenager." She turned to Sharon with a glare and snarled, "Happy now?"

Sharon nodded her approval to Essie.

Hannah stood with the milk jug in one hand and a stunned look on her face. "What did you say?"

Sharon knew Essie would never repeat what she'd said so she offered an explanation. "Essie's been watching the videos and realizes she might not have treated you as nicely as she should have when she was a teenager. She's apologizing to you for being mean. Isn't that nice?"

Slamming the milk jug on the countertop, Hannah went to face Essie across the eating bar. "And you think a silly apology will put everything behind us?"

Sharon drew in a quick breath. This wasn't going as well as she hoped it would. Offered apologies should be accepted and everyone should forgive each other for the hurtful things they'd done. That's how it happened in Christmas movies. Why wasn't that happening here? This was all wrong.

She could do nothing but try to broker peace between the combatants. "Now, girls," she said as jovially as she could, "we have an agreement to get along. Apologies are a good first step. It won't help things if we are hateful and unforgiving to each other."

Hannah looked at Sharon through droopy eyelids. "Don't sprinkle your sugar on me, Miss Favorite-Holiday-of-All. It makes me want to puke."

Sharon's jaw dropped and her eyes widened until the shock of the comment passed and anger took its place. She wanted to smooth things over, and this insolent sister was making it difficult.

She shook her finger at Hannah. "Be nice! Mother wanted us to follow her last wishes, and that's what we're going to do! You can be nice about it, or you can leave and let Essie and me handle it."

Shaking her head, Hannah replied in a tone of determination and higher volume, "Oh no! You're not getting rid of me that easily. I'm not leaving here without my part of the inheritance."

Essie banged her fists on the eating bar. "That settles it. There's no way the three of us can share this house. We're selling it and splitting the money."

Sharon cried out in alarm. "But what about the clock? Mother said not to sell—"

Walking around the end of the eating bar, Hannah stared at her sisters like a cobra about to strike. "I don't care what Mother said. I don't need you two in my life."

Essie's bitter voice behind her frightened Sharon.

"Agreed. Mother's plan failed. I will not be manipulated into liking people who don't like me."

Hannah went nose-to-nose with Essie. "Good. All that's left is to decide who gets the—"

A knock at the door interrupted the sisters mid-fight.

Sharon threw up her hands in disgust, her peacekeeping efforts in rubble. She went to the front door and opened it. A plump, well-dressed woman stood there holding her large bejeweled purse in one hand and a cell phone in the other.

"May I help you?" Sharon asked the overly confident woman.

"Is this where Hannah Headless lives?" The woman tried to look around Sharon into the house. "She told me this place was for sale. I'm a realtor and I'm here to help with that."

Chapter 13

Hannah

Out of view of the doorway, Hannah rushed behind the counter and squatted down. The voice coming from the doorway was one she'd hoped to never hear again. The voice she last heard when she was in the airport. Elvira had found her!

She put her hand over her gaping mouth and stared back at the questioning eyes of Essie who was leaning over the eating bar. She shook her head and mouthed *No no no no!*

From the doorway, she heard Sharon say, "You must be mistaken. This house is not for sale."

Essie joined her sister in the doorway. "What's going on here?"

Elvira let out a squeal of delight. "You must be the other two people she told me about, who don't want to sell this house. I can assure you the time is *perfect* for selling this lovely cottage. May I come in?"

Hannah heard her sisters begin to protest, but the loud clomping of high heels on the hardwood floor signaled the large woman had made her way in. Anger flared in Hannah. She stood up and stepped out of the kitchen to come face to face with Elvira.

Elvira gathered Hannah in a bear hug. "Oh, there you are, sweetie! Good to see you again."

Hannah pushed the woman away from her. Elvira stumbled backward slightly, teetering on her tall heels for a moment. Her large exposed cleavage shook like a mini earthquake as she regained her balance. Her tight floral dress stretched around her large figure and flared out after it passed her hips on its way to her large calves. The soles of the high-heeled shoes broadened out under the weight of the wearer. Her overly large purse hung over her hefty arm.

"You heard my sister," Hannah said brusquely, "the house is not for sale." Her fingernails dug into her palms as she stood ready to defend her stance on the issue. "I was wrong when I said we might sell it."

Elvira quickly opened her purse and pulled out several papers. "I've run comps on this place, and I think you'll be surprised at how they came out. The place needs updating, but it's worth more than you might think."

A screech of joy crossed with greed flew out of Elvira's mouth. "Because it's outdated, it'll take money to fix it before we sell it. But believe you me, you'd make it back." She waved the papers in front of the women.

Hannah glanced at her sisters, who stood behind Elvira. Sharon's frown revealed her position on the matter.

Essie was a different matter. Hannah could see the numbers and money signs pass across Essie's glazed-over eyes as she considered the possibilities. As Essie's mouth began to move, Hannah knew she had only an instant to stop it.

Hannah pushed the papers away. "We're still searching for our mother's last wishes. We haven't found them yet, so it's premature to talk about selling. We'll decide what we're going to do later. As you see, we're not prepared to sell now, but as soon as we are, we'll contact you." Hannah nudged the woman toward the open door.

Setting her feet firmly, Elvira resisted Hannah's efforts to move her back.

She nudged harder with no effect. She could have been pushing against a sleeping elephant.

Elvira gave her a smirk, like this tactic had been tried and failed before. "Now's a good time for me."

Essie snapped out of her trance. "Hannah's right. We're not ready to sell right now. Maybe later." She held the front door open wider, waving the door slightly to lure Elvira toward it.

Hannah put her arm around the large-framed woman and grimaced slightly. The smell of cheap perfume would not easily come out of her outfit.

This time, she succeeded in moving Elvira closer to the exit. "Once we decide what we're going to do, you'll be among the first to know." She smiled with fake sweetness at the woman as she pushed a little harder on her to get her moving faster on her way out.

Elvira shrugged off Hannah, nudging her away. "What can I do to persuade you to list it with me? We could sign the papers now, but I wouldn't execute them until you said I could." She paused.

She pulled another set of papers out of her purse and waved them at the sisters. "I would leave it off the public listing until you make up your mind. Trust me," she said in a singsong voice, "I have connections who would pay a bundle. How about I get the ball rolling."

Hannah wished she could roll this obnoxious female ball of rhinestones out the door. "Not today." She gave one last shove and Elvira stumbled out onto the front porch. "Thanks for calling."

With that, Essie slammed the door.

All was quiet until Elvira shouted through the door, requesting to be let back in. Her high-pitched pleadings came through the door.

Hannah put her fingers in her ears.

After a few eon-long minutes, she said she'd leave her card and the comparisons on the porch for them to look at and to call her at their earliest convenience. Her heavy footsteps on the porch let the sisters know she was walking across it, trying to peek into the windows.

As the sisters huddled together, Sharon whispered, "Glad we haven't opened the curtains yet."

After a few minutes, they heard her lumber off the porch and in another minute, heard her car roar to life. The crunching of gravel announced her departure.

Essie put her hands on her hips and glared at Hannah. "Who was that? Someone you know?"

Hannah threw her hands up in self-defense. "She sat by me on my flight here. I must have mentioned something about selling the house. I didn't know she was a realtor! And I didn't know Mother left it to us or else I wouldn't have said anything."

Putting her hand over her mouth, she looked away. This added complication was no one's fault but her own and she knew it. Plus, she smelled like Elvira and needed a shower immediately.

Sharon walked to the sofa and plopped down. "You know how realtors are. Like pit bulls. Once they bite, they won't let go. Mark my words, she'll be back. And when she comes, she won't be as easy to get rid of. We're on her list of must-haves-at-any-cost."

She reached out and got the remote control. "We need to find Mother's last video as quickly as possible. We know what to do."

The girlhood voices from the video irritated Hannah. The arguments, the pressure to be nice to people she didn't like, the hurry to get home before Halloween was getting to be too much. She exploded verbally. "I can't take this anymore! I'm tired of being cooped up in here for what seems like days. I don't even know what day it is!"

She was mad at herself, at her sisters for being here, at her mother for dying, at Elvira, at everybody in the world. She needed a change of scenery. "I'm going down to the beach to relax a little. You watch the videos all you want. I'm going for a swim." She didn't wait for an answer before spinning around and going down the hallway toward her room to change.

Sharon turned the video machine off, then the TV. "Let's take a trip to town," she yelled out. "You're right. It seems like forever ago that we got here. Besides," she held up the skirt of her long dress, "this thing is hot and I'd like to get something cooler. I told Santa I'd go shopping while I was here."

Hannah went back into the living room. She was tired, smelly, and fed up with being locked in the small house with two women she didn't know well or want to know. Control of her frustration flew away like the gulls out on the beach.

She walked in front of the TV and stopped, one hand on her hip. "Something in red, no doubt. Everything you have is red. You should buy something yellow or orange or black. Something that would knock Santa's fuzzy hat off his head."

Sharon's face got red as she rose from the sofa. "I happen to like red and Santa likes it too. It's much better than wearing all black!" Her volume raised in her defense. "If we're going to talk about wearing different colors, why don't *you* buy something red or yellow or blue."

"Yeah," Essie piped in from the kitchen where she was getting another cup of coffee. "Anything but black. You can watch your husband's eyes bug out so far it'll knock his head off his shoulders and it'll go rolling down the street." She walked in the living room and sat on the end of the sofa.

Hannah felt her face get hot as anger shot through her. No one had the right to insult Headless, least of all her rude sister. She scrunched her hand into a fist and started toward Essie to show her what she thought of her.

Sharon struggled to get up out of the sofa. "Essie! Stop it! That wasn't a nice thing to say. Headless can't help if he has a physical handicap."

A roar of hostility escaped Hannah's lips. "Headless is not handicapped! He's perfectly normal other than his head is not exactly attached like yours and mine are. That's all! He's a warm loving husband and a great father! And he likes to see me in black!" She stabbed her finger at Essie, trying to think of what else to say.

Essie's snicker filled the hostility-filled room.

"It's perpetual funeral clothing. You're always in mourning." She waved her hand down her attire. "You should have multicolor outfits like me. Much prettier style, don't you think?"

"You look like a dork," Hannah said with a snort as she turned away. "And a cheap dork at that. You wear nothing but pale-colored t-shirts and jeans. Look at you now. Pale pink shirt and worn-out jeans. Yesterday you wore the same jeans and a pale blue top. Ever had a bold color or pattern on? Ever wear anything other than jeans and t-shirts? Or cheap polyester suits?"

Sharon got between her glaring sisters. "Remember our truce and quit criticizing each other's wardrobe. Let's go to the mall and Hannah, you can pick out something un-red for me to try on and Essie, you can pick out something un-black for Hannah to try on. And I'll pick something for you, Essie. We don't have to buy the outfit, but we have to try it on to see how we look in other colors."

She looked from one sister to the other. "It's a simple game, but will be fun to try. What do you say?"

Crossing her arms and turning her back, Essie said, "I'm not doing it."

Hannah let out a chortle. "Afraid you'll look good in something other than Easter-egg bland?"

Essie spun around with the fierceness of a hurricane. "Stop insulting me, you—you—you black widow spider! I wear the clothes I can afford and if you don't like it, go—"

"Essie, stop!" Sharon cried out in fear.

"—go jump in the lake!" Essie shouted, her neck veins bulging.

Sharon burst into tears, breaking the tension with her sobbing as she rushed to the sofa and clawed at the tissue box.

Hannah watched her sob into a fist full of tissues and felt like crying herself. This forced confinement had stretched her patience and endurance to the limit. Somehow, she knew she had to find the strength to get through this until her mother's estate was settled. With a slight rill of guilt making its way through her, she let out several heavy sighs to release the pressure inside.

"I'm sorry, Sharon," Hannah said quietly. "I broke the truce. If you want to go shopping, I'll go. And I'll try on any outfit you pick out for me. Also, I apologize to you, Essie—" saying the words was like hacking up a cactus— "for being rude." She stood rubbing the palm of her hand with her thumb, waiting for a response. Any response. Anything to get her out of this uncomfortable situation.

"I'm sorry too, Sharon," Essie said, sniffing. "And to you, Hannah." She went to the overstuffed chair and sat.

Sharon pushed the tissue box toward her and she took one.

Dabbing her eyes, Essie said, "We can go shopping, but I can't afford to buy anything. Money is tight for us right now." With reddened cheeks, she kept her eyes on the tissue, slowly tearing it into pieces.

Sharon let out a small laugh as she dried her tears. "That's okay. Santa gave me a credit card and told me to buy stuff with it. If you find something you like, we'll get it and consider it an early Christmas present."

With a bigger laugh, she wadded her tissues into

a ball and threw them in the wastebasket. "Shopping will be fun. I can't remember the last time I shopped in a store instead of on-line."

Essie shrugged. "Fine. I'll play along, but you'll see I wear the perfect clothes for me." With raised eyebrows, she ran her fingers through her graying hair. "Easter has no complaints about what I wear."

Hannah felt a little of the pressure ease. Shopping together might ease it more. "Fine. We'll choose outfits for each other. Something we want to see the other dressed in. We'll see who's got fashion sense."

"One more thing," Sharon said with a smile. "We have to model them for each other. No fair not showing what it looks like on you."

"Agreed," Hannah said. "But first, I have to go wash that woman's perfume off me!"

Chapter 14

Essie

Essie stared at her images in the three-way mirrors in the tiny dressing room. She closed her eyes to the sight. What had she been thinking when she agreed to play this silly game? Mothers of thirteen didn't wear things like this.

Sharon had chosen something with red in it for her. Red and white chevrons. Thin straps held up the high-waisted bodice, and the A-line skirt went to her ankles. Essie's upper arms, usually hidden under sleeves, looked naked. Like her chest. The v-neckline was much lower than her t-shirts.

She had to admit it made her look thinner, but she'd never buy this dress. First, it would stun Easter and the kids to see her dressed this way. It exposed more skin than she wanted to show. Secondly, she couldn't afford it, even if she wanted it.

Essie opened one eye to see the view again. When she turned to check the side view, the chevrons moved everywhere in the mirrors around her, making her slightly dizzy.

"Time to come out!" Sharon's voice rang out

through the dressing rooms and the thin door shielding Essie from their view. "Don't be chicken. You have to show us how you look."

With her hand on the doorknob, Essie froze. The urge to cover herself with a sweater or a shawl was overwhelming. No one had ever seen her in something like this. Why start now? "I don't think I want to play this game anymore," she said as she started to take off the offensive garb.

Banging on her dressing room door, Hannah yelled, "Come on out. If I have to do this, you do too. You don't look any more ridiculous than me."

"You don't look ridiculous," Sharon replied, letting out a catcall whistle. "You look great in pink."

Essie looked in the mirror again. There was no escape. She might as well get it over with.

Slowly she opened the door and stepped out. Holding her hand over her too-exposed chest, she twirled around for her sisters. Joining in their laughter, she knew she looked as silly as they did.

Essie had chosen a nice dress for Hannah. Pale pink fabric printed with large white and yellow flowers hung loosely around her, hiding her slim figure. The fabric had appealed to Essie which is why she picked it out for Hannah, but seeing the dress on her sister, it lost its appeal. The pink in the fabric made Hannah's face look splotchy and pale. The color didn't suit her at all.

With her hand on her hip and the downturn of her mouth, Hannah looked as miserable as Essie felt in her dress.

With a sign of resignation, Essie admitted to herself that dressing other women was not her forte.

Sharon was wearing the outfit Hannah had

picked out for her: a black culottes set with a matching top. Something she might consider buying, Essie loved the colorful embroidered flowers on the yoke of the jacket. But on Sharon, it looked terrible. She looked paler than ever and her legs were so white Essie almost needed sunglasses to look at them.

Essie decided to settle the matter for them all. "Anyone other than me want to get out of these ridiculous outfits?"

Hannah's arm shot up.

Sharon looked down at her outfit and timidly raised her hand.

Relieved, Essie spoke. "The vote is unanimous. Let's change and shop for ourselves."

Quickly, they changed back into their clothes. As Hannah wandered among the clothes racks outside the dressing room, Essie and Sharon hung the discarded outfits on the reject rack.

Hannah rushed in and pushed them into a changing room. Following them in, she slammed the door behind her. She shushed their protests and told them to keep quiet. Her eyes were wide with excitement or fear. Essie couldn't tell which.

"Elvira is headed this way!" Hannah whispered softly. "I don't want to deal with her again today!"

"Me neither!" Essie said as she noticed Sharon's face pale slightly. Fearful of another panic attack, she knew she had to calm her down. "Let's stay in here until she's in her changing room. We can sneak out without her seeing us."

The sisters nodded as they stood still in the crowded room.

Essie made Sharon look at her as she helped her

with her breathing rhythm. When Sharon stepped on her toe, she quickly covered her mouth to stifle the yelp of pain that would have revealed their presence.

Hannah shushed them as Elvira McKinzor's voice grew louder.

As Elvira came into a dressing room, she snapped her fingers. "Hey saleslady! Hey you!" She snapped her fingers again. "Yeah, you. Why don't you stand by in case I need a different size, okay? Thanks, honey."

The plodding of her heavy feet went by the sisters' door and the slam of the door announced she was in her changing room.

Several grunts and groans were heard until the distasteful sounds were drowned out by Elvira's phone ringing. She answered it immediately. "Hi, sugar. What's that? No, I haven't gone back out to see them. They were adamant about not wanting to sell, but I think I can persuade them otherwise. That crazy woman's house is worth a fortune."

The time had come to sneak away. Essie turned the door knob to look out and seeing the coast was clear, she started out of the small dressing room.

Before she took one step, she felt herself being tugged back in. Hannah quickly shut the door. She waved off their puzzled looks and pointed toward Elvira's voice.

"If we can get it from them before they know that. We subdivide it and build townhouses. We'll be the ones making the fortune. They're all foreigners so they have no idea what they're sitting on. Yes, yes, I'll keep them ignorant. But we have to move fast before anyone else finds out about it."

Hannah looked like she was ready to erupt. She mouthed, *She's talking about us!*

How do you know? Sharon mouthed back.

"Hey saleslady!" Elvira bellowed. "I need this in the next size up!"

The sisters saw a garment arc through the air past the top of their door. They heard the poor saleslady utter a quick 'yes ma'am' before scurrying off.

Elvira resumed her conversation. "Don't worry. I still have some tricks up my sleeve. I'll get them to sell before the week's out. It's easy to fool the clueless."

Hannah pulled them closer and whispered softly. "When we talked on the plane, she called Mother's cottage 'The crazy woman's house.' I'm sure she's talking about us!"

Essie felt her anger rising. That woman dared to call their mother crazy! And dared to presume she could exploit them that way. Tricks up her sleeve? What did that mean?

The saleslady came back quickly and gave Elvira a new set of whatever she had asked for.

Essie hoped she would quickly take whatever she was trying on and leave. They wanted out of the cramped space. Her sore toe was threatened with another mashing in these tight quarters.

Elvira's grating voice came drifting over the wall to them. "I know. We've waited years for that crazy old lady to die, and her stupid daughters are not going to stand in our way."

Sharon's mouth flew open, and Essie quickly covered it with her hand to stop the cry of alarm that would give them away. They had to know more if they wanted to fight Elvira on her own terms.

The sounds of rustling fabric, slight ripping, and a grunt came through the wall. "I know. We've wanted that land too long to wait another day. If they were interested in the place, how come they haven't been around for years? Don't worry. I'll have them begging me to take it. Sugar, I gotta go. I'll see you tonight."

Elvira hung up from whoever she was talking to and filled the air with her off-key humming and grunting as she struggled to get things on.

After a few moments, the sisters heard the door slam and heavy footsteps go past their room.

"Hey saleslady, I didn't like any of it." Elvira must have paraded off because peace returned to the store.

Essie slowly turned the doorknob and peeked out. A saleslady with an armful of clothing looked out of the dressing room at something distasteful to her, judging from her expression. Elvira's voice was nowhere to be heard.

She opened the dressing room door a little wider and looked to make sure the coast was clear before signaling her sisters to follow her out.

Before leaving the area, she felt a tug on her arm and turned to see Sharon waving her to what had been Elvira's dressing room. Clothes were flung everywhere and wadded in balls in the corners. Elvira hadn't bothered to return anything to the hangers, but apparently kicked them off and let them lay where they had fallen.

Essie tsked and pulled Hannah and Sharon toward the door. Together they quickly slipped out the back way, ever watchful for the giant lady who wanted to take their house away from them.

Back at the cottage, Essie sat on the sofa, watching Sharon pace the floor in the living room of the cottage. Hannah sat in the overstuffed chair, watching the scene with half-closed eyes, apparently bored with the drama.

Sharon stopped and looked at her sisters, wild-eyed and frantic. "You heard what she said. She's coming back!" Sharon waved her hands in the air. "And with more tricks up her sleeve! Whatever are we going to do? How can we fend her off?" Her breath came in quick short gasps as she walked in front of the dark TV set.

Fearing Sharon would go into a full-blown panic attack, Essie quickly got a paper bag from the stash of them on the coffee table. Handing one to Sharon, they sat on the sofa together as she coached Sharon into slowing her breathing down, doing what she remembered seeing her mother do for Sharon when her anxiety got out of control.

Essie reassured Sharon they wouldn't let anything happen to the cottage. No one could force them to sign papers or sell the house, no matter what Elvira said.

The paper bag moved in and out more slowly, and Sharon seemed calmer. That in turn made Essie feel calmer.

Hannah tapped her fingertips together. "We have to keep our wits about us if we're going to fend off this old bitty when she comes back. Panicking won't help anything."

"I can't help it!" Sharon cried out, putting the bag over her face again.

Essie shot Hannah a be-nice glare.

Rolling her eyes, Hannah continued in a calmer voice. "I'll say it one more time. They can't force us to sign the house over. We must work together to find a way to make her see we are not selling. I don't want to leave those vultures circling over the house after we go home."

Essie took in a quick breath and covered her mouth with her hand as her heart skipped a beat. She and Easter had talked about selling the cottage to get a new kitchen. They'd only talked about it because they couldn't afford a remodel any other way. She hadn't mentioned their discussion to her sisters and was thankful they didn't know. Besides, she'd changed her mind about it.

She couldn't sell her mother's place to that uncaring, money-hungry goon. Kitchen or no kitchen, she wouldn't sell the house to anyone who was going to sell it off piece by piece. But how could she tell Easter she'd come to that decision?

"Essie!"

Hannah's voice jolted her out of her thoughts.

"What are you thinking about?" Hannah was studying Essie's face. "Something's going on in your head."

Essie felt her face grow hot, afraid she'd have to expose her inner thoughts.

Hannah pressed her. "Come on, come on. Let's hear it. You're thinking of selling, aren't you?"

Sharon grabbed her chest like she was having a heart attack. "You'd sell Mother's house?" Up went the bag again, moving rapidly in and out.

Essie stared at her lap and folded and unfolded the hem of her shirt. She was caught. She would let them know what she'd been thinking.

"If you must know, when Easter and I talked about the house before I left," she took a hard swallow, mostly her pride, "we decided it would be nice to have the money to upgrade our kitchen and other things on our house. So yes, we talked about selling it. At the time, it seemed like a good way to raise money to make things more comfortable for us."

Sharon had put the bag down and was staring at her with narrowed eyes. "So, you *are* thinking of selling."

Not wanting to see her sister's scowl, Essie looked at her hands. "Now that I'm here, I'm not sure I want to sell it. But I'm not sure what we'd do if we kept this place. We can't afford to bring our family over. Plus, we might not be able to pay our share in its upkeep."

Hannah let out a sound of disgust. "I'm getting tired of hearing how poor you are. You use that poverty card every time something comes up. Enough already!"

Anger flashed through Essie like an electrical shock. She sat up straight and pointed at her overbearing sister. "I'm sorry if we're not as well off as you are. I guess Easter and I aren't as good with money as you are, Miss Snob!"

Hannah mimed playing a violin, which only infuriated Essie more.

"You're so self-absorbed —"

"Quiet!" Sharon bellowed like a frustrated teacher in a room of rowdy kids. "Both of you, shut up!"

Stunned at the sudden outburst, Essie and

Hannah followed her command.

Sharon glowered from one to the other. "No more of this. Let's work together to solve the problem. Essie, Hannah and I can buy your part of the cottage. You'd have the money to do what you need to do."

Essie pinched the bridge of her nose and closed her eyes, hoping to conger up control of her emotions. "Before you declare me the enemy, let me continue."

Looking at her sisters' angry faces, she went on. "Now that I'm here, I know this place is too special to let go. That clock—" she waved her hand toward the grandfather clock sitting silently against the wall, "—is magical, like Mother said. It's the real value of the house."

She leaned forward to make her point. "Think of it. We can come here and live for days inside while outside, we've lost no time at all. It's almost like finding the fountain of youth."

Hannah shook her head. "If it were the fountain of youth, Mother would still be living."

Sharon nodded in agreement.

"True," Essie said, rubbing her neck like she often did when she was contemplating deep thoughts. "It's not everlasting time. It's a time alterer. There's no value that can be put on the clock. And there's no price anyone could pay to take away this magical cottage." Essie paused, wondering if Hannah would attack her on that point.

Hannah sat silent, but looked skeptical.

Sharon leaned forward on the sofa and stared at Essie. "Does that mean you're not going to sell?"

Essie nodded.

Sharon threw her wrinkled paper bag into the

air. "Oh, what a relief! If Elvira knew we were divided about selling, she'd have eaten us alive."

Hannah watched with crossed arms from the overstuffed chair, neither smiling nor agreeing. She looked at Essie out of the corner of her eyes, like she wasn't sure she believed her or not. Her look was as black as the faux leather skirt she wore. "I'm not selling. And not you or that fat old realtor can make me sign papers to sell my part of this house."

"Don't be mad, Hannah," Sharon exclaimed. "Essie said she's not interested in selling. That means we're all agreed. We're keeping Mother's house." She looked around and found her paper bag and pulled it close again.

Hannah pointed at Essie. "Make sure you don't change your mind again." She got up and went into her bedroom and slammed the door.

Essie leaned her head against the back of the sofa and closed her eyes. She could hear Sharon breathing in her bag again. She rubbed her stomach that was tied into knots.

Honesty with her sisters had not been the right thing to do. They were back to where they started, distrusting each other. But she felt Hannah knew her better than she cared to admit. She wanted to keep the house, but she needed the money. Hannah was right to doubt her decision.

She'd have to call Easter and tell him about her decision to keep the house despite needing the money for home repairs. He wouldn't be mad, but he'd be disappointed in her reversed decision without consulting him first. He might try to talk her out of it.

She turned her head to look at the silent clock.

This was her mother's house and her clock. The magical clock. That's what made the house worth keeping. That's why she had to tell Easter there would be no money for remodeling.

Chapter 15

Sharon

Sharon stared out the kitchen window as she washed the last of the dirty dishes. Hannah had gone to the beach, and Essie was in her room talking with Easter. She hoped he wouldn't change Essie's mind about selling. The thought turned her insides to mush. She reached for a bowl to stir up another batch of cookies.

Baking was her therapy when she felt stressed by circumstances out of her control. Bake...and bake more...and more. Bake until the whole kitchen was full of breads, pies, cookies, and cakes.

Essie walked into the kitchen after a cookie sheet was pulled from the oven. "The house smells wonderful, Sharon," she commented as she took a bite of a snickerdoodle cookie baked earlier. "These are delicious!" She got another without finishing the first one.

Sharon smiled while she continued to work. "It's how I relax. It controls my anxiety."

Waving her hand, Essie spoke with her mouth full, "What are you going to do with this? We can't eat it all, and the freezer isn't big enough to hold it."

Sharon stopped what she was doing and looked around. Every flat surface held something. Cakes, cookies, or pies, with two loaves of fresh bread in the corner. She'd been so deep in thought she'd lost track of how much she'd made.

"Oh dear! At home, Santa and the elves eat it all, but here, I don't know what I'll do with it!"

Essie laughed as she picked out a different kind of cookie to try. "I'm happy to taste it, but I shouldn't be eating too much of this sweet goodness. I wonder if we could donate it to the foodbank or something?"

"I don't think they take homemade food, just ingredients. Maybe there's nursing homes or homeless shelters that would take it. I would hate for it to go to waste."

Essie sniffed the steam coming off the fresh cookies. She sat on a stool by the eating bar. "I'll make some phone calls while you get it ready to transport."

Sharon called after Essie as she turned to go. "What did Easter say? Is he upset you want to keep the house?" Her heart pounded loudly. She might not get the answer she wanted to hear.

Essie turned back to face her sister. "He's fine with it, and understands why I changed my mind."

"Does he support us in keeping it?"

"Yes, he does. No need to worry." She left the kitchen, leaving Sharon to wonder if she was telling the truth or not.

That afternoon, the sisters drove to the homeless shelter that was excited to get Sharon's baked goods. The people at the shelter embraced them and thanked them profusely. When they left, smiling faces and warmed hearts filled the car.

Sharon felt good inside. Essie's confession about wanting to sell the house had threatened to tear them apart again, but her baking had brought them back together. Donating her work to those less fortunate had made her sisters see what good they could accomplish together. All she had to do was maintain the peace.

On the way back to the cottage, they stopped at a grocery store to get more baking supplies. Sharon felt a little guilty for using everything that was there when they arrived, plus the items Mr. Howard brought. Her therapy was getting expensive.

Together they'd decided to renew their efforts to find their mother's last video in the stacks remaining in the closet. They'd watched quite a few, but there were still piles to go. They'd have to set the clock to five to have time to get it done.

Hannah kept talking about having to go home soon so she could be with Headless for their holiday. Sharon couldn't fault her for that. She'd feel the same way if Christmas was quickly approaching.

Driving to the house, Sharon was surprised to see a long black car in the driveway and two men sitting on their porch. Essie quickly parked the car, and they got out.

Mr. Howard stood as they hurried up the porch steps. "Good afternoon, ladies! I hope you don't mind me dropping in. This is my good friend, Ed Johnson." Ed shook the ladies' hands, leaving behind a slight dampness on their palms.

Sharon's hand felt repulsive. She held it out to the side until she could wash it.

Mr. Howard rocked back and forth on his feet and fumbled with large suspenders under his light suit jacket. He waved away a fly that seemed determined to land on his large nose. "I wanted to stop by and see how things were going. Have you come to a decision about this old house?"

Sharon's blood ran hot. The way he said it made her see he had little respect for them or their mother. He was out to take advantage of them.

Essie spoke first. "We're still reviewing the tapes she left for us. We'll let you know as soon as we decide what to do."

Mr. Howard and Mr. Johnson exchanged glances. "You see, I have your mother's official will, which I read to you ladies a few days ago. As you know, the deed was transferred to you. You own this place."

Sharon was resisting the urge to tell the man to get off their porch and off their property, but held back the fire on the tip of her tongue. "Yes, we do. What's your point?"

"Mr. Johnson here is my realtor and he's interested in helping you ladies out by taking this place off your hands. I know you live all over the world. It's silly for you to keep this place. Like I promised your daddy, I'm here to help in any way I can."

Simultaneously, the three sisters crossed their arms. "It's not for sale," Sharon said before the others could say the same thing.

Mr. Howard and Mr. Johnson let out the fake laughter of scoundrels. "You can't be serious, ladies," Mr. Johnson said. "Why, the taxes on this place are sky high. Why pay for that when you won't get to enjoy it much?"

"You heard my sister, Mr. Howard," Hannah

said, slightly growling, "it's not for sale." She took a step toward the man, uncrossed her arms, and stood with clenched fists and a wanna-piece-uh-me scowl on her face.

Small beads of sweat broke out across Mr. Howard's forehead before he broke into a nervous laugh. "No need for things to get ugly here." He took another step back and lightly pushed Mr. Johnson ahead of him.

A look of fear flashed across Mr. Johnson's face as he took a step back. A broad grin spread across his mouth, but it didn't continue into his eyes. "Of—of course not! We're here trying to help. I can guarantee you a good price for it." He turned and gave Mr. Howard a what-do-we-do-now grimace.

Mr. Howard smoothed his tie across his belly that rivaled Santa's in size. "Yes. We wanted to let you know you aren't stuck with this place and if you ever think of selling it, please give me a call. Right, Ed?"

Ed sidled toward the porch steps. "Right, Howie. Good day, ladies." Mr. Johnson quickly turned and hightailed it back to the car.

Mr. Howard watched his friend leave, then turned back to the ladies. "I hope you'll at least consider selling. Let me know." He tipped an imaginary hat to them before he turned to go.

Sharon hated for anyone to go away mad, even those she didn't like. "Mr. Howard," she said in her sweetest voice.

The man stopped and stared at her, a slight longing in his eyes gave away his hopes. The breeze blew his comb-over the other direction, making it stand up like a waving hand out of the top of his head.

Stifling a giggle, Sharon gave him a smile that belied her true anger behind it. "Thanks for coming. Have a safe trip back." She gave a little wave with her fingertips.

The man's shoulders slumped and he nodded. "I guess we'll do this the hard way," he muttered as he plodded to his car. "Time for Plan B," he mumbled softly, but Sharon heard it.

She turned to her sisters. "I must call Santa. I have two more names for our naughty list." She tittered as she walked past them into the house. "Only coal in their stockings this Christmas!"

Chapter 16

Hannah

Sitting in the overstuffed chair, Hannah dug through the folder Mr. Howard had given the ladies at their first meeting, looking for answers to nagging questions. Sharon was baking again, and Essie sat on the sofa, rubbing the tension out of her temples.

Hannah pulled out the deed to the house and read it closely. A knot formed in her stomach with her worry about whether Mr. Howard had processed the deed correctly. His parting words filled her with dread. He might have left a loophole somewhere in it.

Essie straightened and organized several papers out of the folder and started to examine them. "What do you hope to find?" she asked softly.

Without looking up, Hannah replied, "I'm looking for anything he might use to take the house away from us."

Sharon came out of the kitchen, with flour on her cheek and down the front of her apron. "But why would he do that? Oh right, money." She let out a resigned sigh. "He must have fooled Mother into thinking he was honest."

Essie glanced over several papers. "Greed turns people into scoundrels very easily. Sadly, it happens a lot. That's why your naughty list keeps getting longer and longer."

Wiping her face with the back of her hand, Sharon replied, "I see it all the time. The world is much more materialistic, and greed for wealth and possessions is taking over. It's reflected in the letters we get every year. It's no surprise Mr. Howard has turned to dishonesty to accumulate more." Her voice broke with her last words.

Hannah turned to look at her sister who had tears in her eyes. She looked at the sister without the tears who handed her the tissues to pass along.

Hannah put the papers down and massaged her fists trying to relax. She took a deep breath and exhaled the building stress. They didn't have time for panic and tears. Mr. Howard was out to steal the house from them, and they needed a plan to stop him.

Feeling slightly calmer and more in control, she told her sisters, "We need to figure out what Mr. Howard's ploy is to take the house so we can prevent it. We don't have much time to plan. I must be home by Halloween. That's only eleven days away."

She pointed to the silent clock. "Sharon, why don't you set the clock for five o'clock. Let's use it to our advantage."

Sharon stuffed her damp tissue in her apron pocket and went to the clock. Soon the sound of its ticking filled the room.

Essie seemed restless. "Mother's last video will give us a clue. Maybe she knew Mr. Howard was a shyster, and can tell us what we can do to stop him."

Hannah nodded. "She was too smart to be taken in by him. Why don't you and Sharon put on more videos while I look through these papers. I'm no lawyer, but I can read. There may be something in the fine print that will tell us what he's got in mind."

Sharon went to get snacks ready for their long session. Essie came back with a stack of videos and started the first one.

Four videos later, bread crusts and cookie crumbs covered the large platter in the middle of the coffee table. Sharon had her feet propped on the sofa and her back against the arm. She snored softly as the video played scenes of her mother teaching her to dance.

Essie stared blankly at the video, occasionally trying to fast forward through the tapes. The function still didn't work, but the hope remained.

Hannah was busy at work. She pored over the deed, reading the fine print that was truly fine. The small fonts strained her eyes and were beginning to give her a headache. She put the deed in her lap and rubbed her eyes.

Essie came out of her TV trance. "Find anything?"

Hannah shook her head. She noticed Essie looked as tired as she felt. Apparently slowing time didn't relieve the need for rest.

"Nothing. Just a bunch of mumbo jumbo, but nothing too earth-shattering. Want to look at it?" She held the papers out.

Essie waved them off. "If you can't understand it, I know I won't." Adjusting her posture on the sofa, she stretched out her feet on the coffee table. "I admire you for being the smart one in the family. You got all the brains and I was jealous of that sometimes."

Hannah's heart skipped a beat, whether from shock at being given a compliment or surprise at being told she was smart, she couldn't tell for sure. Both were rare. Either alone would have surprised her.

Her face must have betrayed her thoughts because Essie continued, "Why are you surprised? You know you're the smart one."

Hannah recovered and shook her head. "No, I'm not! You're the one who made the best grades in school. You're the brain in the family, and I'm the bulldog, as Mother called it. Tenacious. That's what I am."

Essie laughed softly. "I'll give you that one. She said you never let go of an idea." She ran her hand through her mussed hair and yawned. "I might have been the smart one back then, but I've lost intelligence with refereeing feuding children. Doesn't leave much time for reading and stuff like that."

Hannah tossed the deed papers on the coffee table and sat back in the chair. "How do you do it? Thirteen kids? I have my hands full with two boys. When do you have time to breathe?"

"Organization and chore lists. Couldn't live without them." Essie curled up on the sofa, pushing Sharon's feet out a little.

Sharon's soft snoring was interrupted until she found a comfortable spot again. It resumed when she got still.

A look of total contentment covered Essie's tired face. "We didn't plan to have so many kids. It took only six pregnancies to amass our mob. But I wouldn't trade any of them for anything in the world. I love my life."

Hannah felt a twinge of amazement hit her heart like a blow dart. All this time, she'd pitied Essie for being burdened with a huge family. She knew they struggled to make ends meet. The egg factory provided enough to live on, but nothing extra. Donations for Easter eggs were not common nor were they very big. She could understand why Essie might want to sell the house.

Essie's eyes narrowed. "What are you thinking? Don't pity me! I don't like that!"

Hannah held up her hands in surrender. "That's not what I was thinking. I like hearing you love your life. I guess I've never heard you say it. I'm a little surprised."

Essie cocked her head. "Surprised I'm happy?"

Hannah laughed softly. "I assumed anyone with that many kids wouldn't be too happy. My mistake."

Essie gave her a face that conveyed her irritation. Hannah quickly said, "I was wrong. I admit it. I'm sorry." That softened her sister's face.

"Thanks." Essie's eyes got a little misty.

"Such a sweet moment!" Sharon crooned.

Essie and Hannah jumped in fright.

Sharon sat up with a huge grin on her face. "I'm glad I heard it! Sisters liking each other again! How I love it! Why, I might put you back on the Good List." She let out a cackle and clapped her hands.

"Sharon!" Hannah put a hand on her wildly beating heart. "I thought you were sleeping! You scared me!"

Sharon laughed. "You two need to learn the difference between fake snoring and real snoring. If I were really snoring, the roof would be rattling."

The video sound came on louder as they heard their mother laughing and saying, "You silly girl!"

Chills ran through Hannah. It was almost like Mother was here watching them. She picked up the remote and turned the video machine off.

An eerie quiet enveloped the women, with nothing but the ticking clock making a sound. None of them dared to move. Hannah's heart was beating so rapidly and loudly she was afraid her sisters could hear it. Daring to break the spell, she whispered, "That was spooky!"

Sharon looked around the them. "She must be haunting this place."

Hannah dismissed the idea. "Relax. I'm used to haunted houses, and this one's not haunted. Still, it's ironic Mother speaks to us from the videos."

Sitting wide-eyed, Essie stared at the TV. Sharon grabbed for a paper bag.

Amused, Hannah yawned and stretched. "I'm bushed. Let's leave the clock where it's at. We can sleep with time slowed down so we won't lose time on the outside."

Essie stood to go. "Are you sure we should? We age in this time-place or whatever you want to call it. We might look older when we're out there in the other time-place when we stop the clock."

Hannah's mind whirled with fatigue and confusion. What was Essie trying to say? Other time-place? What did that mean? Right now, she didn't care. "It didn't hurt Mother."

Essie opened her mouth to argue, but Hannah cut her off.

"Let's do it this once. We set the clock when it

was morning. We'll be out of sync with the right time on the outside. Let's set the kitchen timer so we awaken at the same time. We'll be more careful about getting rest. We'll not overuse the time-altering thing. Moderation is always best."

The sisters agreed and went to bed, leaving the clock ticking in the living room.

Chapter 17

Essie

Essie walked through the quiet living room, following the aroma of breakfast. The clock sat quietly against the wall, having been stopped by an earlier riser.

Sharon bustled around the kitchen, pulling out the butter and jelly for toast. On the stove, a pan of bacon and eggs sat waiting to be eaten.

Hannah walked in behind Essie and poured a cup of coffee for Essie and another for herself. "It smells delicious, Sharon. You're quite the cook."

Sharon smiled as she set the table. "I love kitchen work. It's my therapy for stress." She looked up quickly. "Not that I'm stressed, but it helps me keep my panic under control."

"I'm happy to have someone else do the cooking," Essie said as she sat down at the table. For the first time in a long while, she felt at ease around her sisters. Last night's breakthrough with Hannah had lifted her spirits, and she felt a smile on her face as she took the coffee from Hannah.

Sharon set a platter of bacon and eggs and a

stack of pancakes in the middle of the table. "I'm not used to cooking for just a few," she said. "I usually cook for a crowd, with Santa and the elves. Of course, I get lots of help from some of the elves. They cook better than I do sometimes." Her eyes glazed over as she stared into space.

Essie understood. "We're all a little homesick."

Sharon blinked and went back to the kitchen. She took plates from the cabinet and set them on the table as she waved for Hannah to sit down.

As Sharon joined the others at the table, Essie held her hands out. Sharon took her hand and reached out for Hannah's.

Hannah looked confused.

"At our house, we say grace before meals," Essie said softly.

Sharon nodded in agreement.

Hannah gingerly reached out and took a hand from each sister.

Essie didn't watch to see if she bowed her head. It didn't matter. She prayed for her sisters, bowed head or not.

"Lord, thank you for this food and bless it to our nourishment. Thank you for our families and bless us all. And please bless all who are less fortunate. Amen."

Sharon beamed. "Lovely. Dig in!"

After breakfast, Essie went out to the beach. The warm white sand felt good between her toes, but stuck to her heavily sun-screened limbs. She tied her sunhat a little tighter as the ocean breeze tried to lift it off her head. She walked down to the water and let the waves wash over her feet, cooling them off.

Hannah was in the deeper water swimming and

snorkeling, something she'd done since she was little.

Essie had never liked the water much. She loved to wade and play in the sand, but deep water scared her silly. She'd seen the movie *Jaws* as a girl, and it scared her so badly she decided never to venture far from shore again.

She thought about Easter and their conversation about keeping the house. He told her he understood and to do what she thought best, but his voice betrayed his disappointment. He supported her whatever the decision, and she loved him the more for it.

Hearing his voice and the kids clambering to talk to her had made her homesick. Somehow, they had to find their mother's last video soon. She had a large family who needed her back as fast as she could get there.

She sat in the sand and filled a plastic bag full of the white stuff. The kids would have fun sticking their hands in it and letting it fall between their fingers. The sample bag might be as close as they ever got to this place. In fact, this might be her last trip back. She wiped a tear away.

Laying back on the sand under a large umbrella, she pulled her sunhat over her face. She'd told Hannah she was happy with her life, but she hadn't told the whole truth. She wished they had more money. She didn't wish for a lot more money. Just enough to take her large family on a trip like this one. Enough to allow her children to see the ocean and play in white sand. In the warm, white sand and sunshine of her childhood home.

Memories. She'd been reliving them since she'd arrived here. They were sweet memories of her mother's care and love for her girls. Like she was passing on to her own children. They would have their own long-lasting memories.

She got up and moved out into the waves until her knees were covered. The waves came in, trying to push her backwards. Despite their efforts, she stayed rooted firmly to the bottom and withstood the waves.

She smiled. She'd do like the waves and stand her ground. There'd be no selling of the house. It was too special, too full of memories, too magical to let someone else live there. Somehow, someway, someday, she'd bring her family here.

Hannah was floating toward her with the surf, her long dark hair streaming out behind her. "Penny for your thoughts."

Essie walked out of the surf and took a seat under the umbrella. Hannah joined her there while she dried with a towel.

"I told Easter I didn't want to sell the cottage. He was disappointed, but understood."

Hannah put the towel down. "Did you tell him why we have to keep it?"

Staring at the blue water, Essie replied, "I didn't tell him about the clock. I didn't want to tell him over the phone. Instead, I was going to argue memories last longer than a new kitchen, but he didn't give me a chance. He agreed before I could say anything. And that's another reason why I love him."

Hannah laughed softly as she laid back on the sand beside Essie. "I thought he was the ugliest man I ever saw when you first brought him home. I was repulsed by the thought of you being married to him. But I must say, he's been gracious and polite almost to a fault. He's got a good heart. I can see why you married him, but I still have a hard time looking at him."

A shall-we-compare-stories giggle came out of Essie. "You want to talk about how husbands look? Shall I tell you what I thought when I first saw Headless?"

Hannah laughed and invited her to share.

"When I first saw Headless take off his—ahem—head, I went in the bathroom and threw up."

"What? You didn't!" Hannah chuckled lightly, but grew sober. "He didn't want any secrets between me and my family. He felt it best everyone knew the truth right off the bat."

"Back then, I couldn't stand to look at him. When you talked about feeding him through a tube while his head was off, I nearly threw up again. How could you love something like that?"

The mental picture of the process caused her to pause to allow her suddenly queasy stomach to settle. She pushed the picture out. "I could see why he loved you, but for the life of me, I couldn't imagine what you saw in him. When you introduced him to the family, he was a gentleman in his ways, and it was as plain as the crab crawling on the sand you loved each other."

"He knew you didn't like him. He tried to avoid you. With the wedding and all..." Hannah's voice trailed off.

Essie blinked hard to keep tears from leaving her eyes. She'd acted like a cad. "I'm sorry. I ruined your special day."

"You didn't ruin it. We still got married, but you put a damper on it."

A tear dropped on Essie's arm, and she quickly wiped it away. "I was shocked at the setting and overreacted to everything."

"The chapel was dark because Headless didn't want people to be uncomfortable. I wore black because it's his favorite color. Did you know black is not the absence of color? It's the presence of all colors in one place. That's why we love it so much."

Essie stared at the grains of sand in front of her. Some moved in the breeze and others stayed firm. Like the grains of sand blown about by the wind, she'd let her emotions blow her away from her family. She'd made a fool of herself on Hannah's wedding day.

Her heart ached with guilt. By rights, Hannah should hate her, but here they sat, sharing secrets. Just like sisters. She couldn't blink hard enough to keep more tears from leaving her eye.

Awash in regret over her past actions, she whispered as she reached over and squeezed Hannah's still-wet hand, "I'm sorry. It never occurred to me Headless was being thoughtful with the dim lights. And I never thought much about the color black, but I should have known it. I've seen my kids use crayons to color in the same spot. The waxy mess turns black. It makes my behavior seem even more dreadful."

Hannah pushed sand around with her hand as she shook her head. "It's all water—"

A sound came from the direction of the cottage, and they turned toward it. They watched as Elvira bumbled her way up the porch steps to knock on the front door.

The two looked at each other with wide eyes and said together, "She's back!"

Chapter 18

Sharon

While her sisters were on the beach, Sharon called Santa to relate how things were going. He encouraged her to help everyone to forgive and make amends. Sharing the house with her sisters wouldn't be a problem if they got along.

Santa asked if she'd had any panic attacks. She assured him Essie had helped her when they came along.

He said the elves were filling in for her quite nicely. She felt a little sad hearing she wasn't missed all that much, but Santa reassured her they would be glad when she returned.

She didn't tell him how much she missed the elves, especially Elwina and Martha, and wondered if they missed her. They made such a good team when cooking for those who worked hard to take care of the reindeer, those who took care of their home complex, and those who made toys.

After she hung up, she sat on the sofa, feet on the coffee table and a cookie in her hand. Everyone at the North Pole worked for the good of everyone else.

Their little community bonded together with the mission of making people happy.

She left that happy home to deal with her feuding sisters. It had been hard on her. She was ready to go home, but cooking and eating took her mind off being homesick.

After starting another video playing, Sharon went to the kitchen to clean and prepare a small luncheon. She'd barely started when the doorbell rang. She dried her hands as she peeked out the front window to see who was disturbing her peace and quiet.

Her heart nearly stopped when she saw the large form of Elvira on the doorstep. She hid in the kitchen. If she didn't answer, Elvira might go away. Sharon didn't think she could handle the overbearing woman alone. Who knew when her sisters would come back from the beach, especially if they were swimming in the surf.

Sharon heard the doorknob turn and the door open. Hannah and Essie hadn't locked the door when they left. Her breath was quickening as fast as her heart was racing.

"Yoo hoo! Anybody home?" Elvira's grating high-pitched voice echoed through the living room where a video was playing on the machine. "Yoo hoo!"

Sharon heard her mother's voice on the video say, "Where do you think you're going?"

She peeked around the corner at the TV, half expecting to see her mother's image pointing a finger at Elvira. Instead, it showed her mother running to catch toddler Hannah as she hurried down the sidewalk. The sight convinced her Hannah's assessment of the house was not correct. Their mother *was* haunting it.

She heard a heavy footstep on the floor as Elvira

muttered, "I might have a little looksee around." The words spurred Sharon to action.

Sharon rushed out of the kitchen into the living room, her voice fired with anger at the intrusion. "What are you doing inside my house? You were not invited in!" Rolling a damp towel as she stared at Elvira, she was ready to inflict a powerful sting with it if she needed to.

Elvira backed toward the door. "Excuse me! I didn't know anyone was home. I rang the doorbell." Her sandaled feet with the bright orange pedicured toes took a step back. Her white power suit had a sparkling purple scarf twisted around the collar.

"And you think it's okay to come in without permission? I want an answer to my question. Why are you in here?"

Elvira set her expensive, over-large bag down on the floor by the front door. "I have news I thought you might need to know." She looked around. "Are your sisters here?"

"Yes, we're here!" Hannah said as she came in the front door wrapped in a towel, still sandy from laying on the beach. She pushed her way past Elvira.

Essie was close behind her. Both were out of breath from running from the beach. Their feet left sandy footprints across the hardwood floor. "What's going on?"

Sharon felt her strength return and slowed her breathing on her own. "Elvira here barged in the house without being asked. Said she'd have a look around." The three sisters stared at the woman who readjusted the scarf hanging across her broad bosom.

With a broad smile, the broad woman said, "Oh

good! You're all here." She cleared her throat and reached for her bag. "I have information here I thought you might be interested in."

She dug through her voluminous purse and pulled out a notepad. "I happened to be at the courthouse looking at something, and guess what I discovered. It seems taxes on this place are in arrears. Several years, in fact. I'm surprised it hasn't been auctioned off yet."

Sharon covered her mouth with her hand and took a step back. Unpaid taxes? Someone else could pay the taxes and take the house away from them. They could lose the house.

"How much do we owe?" she asked softly.

Elvira cleared her throat and checked her little notepad again. "I don't have the exact amount, but it's over $18,000." She closed the notepad with a dramatic flair and threw it into her bag. "Maybe more."

Sharon wasn't the only one who let out a gasp. She saw her sisters stiffen. Essie swayed slightly, and Sharon reached out to steady her.

Hannah seemed to grow larger and blacker. "Get out." Taking a step closer to Elvira, she said louder, "Get out now!"

Elvira backed against the front door.

Years with Santa had taught Sharon how to be jolly and sweet even when she wanted to wring someone's neck. She grabbed Hannah and pulled her back. Smiling as sweet as her sugar cookies, she asked her sister, "How did this issue happen to come up at this particular time?"

Elvira stood away from the door and straightened her scarf again. She gave them a pretentious smile that made Sharon's blood boil. "You should do your homework. It's public record down at the courthouse."

Forget about being sweet! "And why were you looking at such information? Did the book happen to fall open to the page with our house on it?"

Out of the corner of her eye, Sharon saw Hannah tense, ready to spring like a cat on a mouse. She touched her lightly and hoped she'd keep her tongue for now.

Elvira tossed her head. "I thought you might still consider selling this house, and I wanted to do background checks on it."

She held her hands up in front of her. "It's not like I'm the one who didn't pay. All I know is back taxes are owed on this place. The process for collecting the taxes hasn't been started yet, but it could at any time. All someone has to do is pay the back taxes, and the place is theirs."

Sharon's head started swirling again, and her breath came short and quick. She looked around for a paper bag, but seeing none, she held her breath for a second. Her head cleared a little. The anger she was feeling was giving her strength to fight for what was hers.

Essie tossed her sunhat on the overstuffed chair. "Thanks for letting us know," she said calmly. "We'll take care of it right away. Now if you'll excuse us—"

Elvira motioned for everyone to calm down. "But I have a proposal!"

Hannah stepped forward and pushed her toward the door.

Elvira swatted at Hannah's hands as she resisted

the push. "Listen to me for a minute. I think I have a way to make all of us happy. I'll pay the back taxes and you can sell the house to me. That way, you'll get your considerable equity out of the house, and I'll make a little money too. See, we all come out smelling sweet."

Circling her hands as if summoning an answer, she looked at the sisters. "Win win."

"Get outta here!" Hannah hissed.

Sharon held her breath for a moment longer to keep the dizziness at bay. "We're not selling to you or anyone else. We're keeping the house. Time for you to go. Good-bye."

Sharon followed Hannah's example and gave the woman a shove.

"But—but—" Elvira stammered as she stumbled backwards.

Essie stepped forward to reach around Elvira and get the doorknob.

Hannah reached down and picked up the bag. Judging by the strain showing on her arm as her muscles bulged, it wasn't an easy feat. She shoved the bag against Elvira's middle, pushing the woman out onto the porch.

"But—but—"

Sharon stepped forward. "That's our final word. We're keeping the house. Good-bye!"

With a flick of the wrist, Essie slammed the door on the still stuttering woman.

Chapter 19

Hannah

Hannah watched as Essie helped Sharon with her paper bag. She could barely rein in her own fury. She paced and pounded her fist into the other hand.

Good thing Elvira wasn't there or she would have beat her up. She stopped in her tracks. Horace once told her he wanted to beat someone up. She'd had a long talk with him about not wishing harm on others. She loosened her fists and stretched her fingers out.

Thinking a cold shower might help with her fiery temper, she excused herself and ran to her bedroom.

Later, sitting in the overstuffed chair in her black tank top and black shorts, she picked up the deed papers again. She'd read it thoroughly and everything seemed standard. She dug through the other papers she hadn't looked at yet. There might be something in them. She quickly scanned through several.

"We have to pay those taxes. Today!" Sharon cried out before putting the bag back up to her face. She breathed another time or two before adding, "I don't know about you two, but we don't have that kind of money lying around. But we can't let that woman or Ol' Howie pay them first!"

Essie patted her knee, watching the bag go in and out, in and out. "Mother didn't have that much in her bank account, but we'll figure out something. Won't we, Hannah?" Essie's wrinkled brow and questioning eyes tweaked Hannah's heart.

The question scared Hannah. They wanted her to do something. But what? She had no ideas on where to do from there.

She tried to calm her sisters with a fake smile. "Sure we will. Mother didn't leave us a house just to lose it to tax debt—" Her breath caught in her throat. "Wait a minute! Didn't the lawyer tell us all of Mother's debts were paid? I'm sure he did! He said everything had been taken care of, and she owed nothing."

The paper bag went down into Sharon's lap. "Yes, he did! So that means—"

"One of them is lying," Essie finished. "Either Mr. Howard lied or Elvira did. If the taxes are truly not up-to-date, we need to know."

"Yes, we do," Hannah said as she shuffled through the papers on the coffee table. "And when we do, we'll know who is responsible for the oversight. There's got to be a clue in the videos or these papers. We need to redouble our efforts to find the answers." She gave another smile to her sisters to hide her fear.

Hannah picked up the large stack of papers from the coffee table. Other than looking through all of them, she didn't know what else to do.

She and Headless had put money back for the boys' college funds, but it wasn't enough to cover the taxes. She knew Essie didn't have any money, but she wasn't sure about Sharon. Christmas was the richest holiday of all. Surely Sharon had money to pitch in to save the house.

She turned on the floor lamp beside the overstuffed chair. Taking the top sheet of paper, she quickly scanned through it. It was an agreement with a local fellow about checking the house when no one was there. She made a mental note to call the person listed in the agreement and ask about what it would cost them to continue that service after they went home.

Sharon jumped up from the sofa. "I feel the need to bake!" She ran off toward the kitchen.

Essie shrugged. "Whatever makes her feel better." She pointed at the papers scattered on the table. "Want help going through those?"

The pile of papers, the tall stack of unviewed videos, and the short time to get it all done prodded Hannah into action. "I'll go through the papers. Why don't you go through videos. We must find the one where Mother tells us what she wants." She let out a growl. "I'm mad at her for leaving us in this mess."

While one video played, Essie hauled all the videos out of the closet and stacked them on the coffee table. She sorted the ones they'd already seen from the ones still needing reviewed.

Hannah gathered the stack of papers on one end of the coffee table while Essie went through the videos on the other end.

The aroma of cookies wafted into the living room, making Hannah's stomach growl softly. Hannah tried to ignore her sisters and the prodding of her hunger. The pressing issue of unpaid taxes kept her attention focused on the papers.

There were right-of-way papers for the driveway, a living will, papers giving her father medical power of attorney, and a copy of her written will leaving the house and any remaining money to her daughters, to be split equally. An accounting of her debts and assets would be given by an accountant with the firm of Assets, Inc. of Sarasota.

An accounting firm? Mr. Howard hadn't mentioned it. If the firm could give an accounting of Mother's affairs, they must have handled money on her behalf or figured her income taxes or knew something about her finances. She wondered if this is their missing link.

"Hey, girls, we have something to explore. Did Mother ever mention having an accountant?"

Sharon came in from the kitchen, her apron covered in flour.

Essie stopped piling tapes and came to look over Hannah's shoulder. "We never talked about that kind of thing. Why? What did you find?"

Hannah handed the document to Essie and pointed out the paragraph. While she read it, Hannah explained it to Sharon who said, "Do you think they were supposed to pay the property taxes, but didn't?"

Hannah shrugged. "Good accountants would at least track the taxes. This gives us a place to start. Let's call and make an appointment to talk to them today."

A smile came over Sharon's face, and Hannah knew there'd be no more cookies baked that day. Hope had been restored.

Early that afternoon, the sisters sat in the spartan office of Zoe Bergman, accountant and owner of Assets,

Inc. Atop her large walnut desk were her computer, a mouse, a keyboard, and a phone. Behind her was a large credenza and bookcase holding three books and a box of tissues. The sterility of her office décor reflected the lack of personality in the woman who sat behind the desk.

Ms. Bergman sat straight and stiff behind the massive desk, a small figure of a woman for such a large piece of office furniture. Her face looked like a smile had never been there. Her glasses sat on the end of her nose as she peered over the top of them at the women in her office.

With the voice of a hawk screeching as it celebrated a kill, she asked, "What can I do for you?"

Essie and Sharon had given the job of speaking to Hannah. She took the lead.

"Our mother, Francis Time, recently passed away. We understand your firm was supposed to give an accounting of our mother's financial affairs to her lawyer, Howie Howard." Hannah paused, expecting a response of some sort.

Instead Ms. Bergman stared at her without moving or blinking. Hannah wondered if she should wave a hand in front of her face to see if anyone was home. Finally, the thin bespectacled woman blinked, the only sign she was still conscious.

Hoping to egg a response out of the cold woman, Hannah explained more. "Mr. Howard failed to give us those documents. We'd like to get a copy of them. We'd like to settle her affairs as quickly as possible."

Hannah raised her eyebrows, hoping to convey she was through and it was time for the other woman to contribute to the conversation.

The hawkish woman cleared her throat. "Mr. Howard has the documents. You should ask him for them." Nothing but the woman's mouth moved.

Tilting her head slightly, Hannah looked at the woman, wondering if her head would fall off if she moved it. Maybe she was a robot, lacking feeling of any kind. Or maybe she was a distant cousin of Headless and couldn't move her head for fear of it rolling off her shoulders. Maybe he wasn't the only one of his kind on earth.

Essie edged her way into the conversation. "We need information specifically about our mother's finances. We learned she may not have paid the taxes on the cottage. Do you know anything about this? Weren't you supposed to pay them?"

Hannah thought she saw the slightest crack in the armor of this woman. Her eyes widened slightly, and her upper lip became a little moist. Essie had struck a nerve.

She pressed the issue. "We need to know why the property taxes weren't paid on the cottage. Did our mother give you money to pay the taxes? If so, why didn't you pay them?"

Ms. Bergman turned to her computer and typed something in. "Let me pull that account up. This may take a few minutes."

To Hannah, it seemed she typed in more information than might be necessary to pull up an account. One thing was for certain, her mother's name didn't have as many letters in it as she was typing. She felt her blood heat with anger. Something suspicious was going on here, and she didn't like it.

Hannah leaned over to get lip gloss out of her purse. She rubbed a little on her palms. Leaning forward, she put her arms on the large desk. Ms. Bergman turned slightly to look at her. Hannah drug her hands across the polished surface, leaving handprints and smeared lip gloss.

Ms. Bergman's eyes and mouth widened slightly as she stared at the smudges on her otherwise spotless desk.

For a moment, Hannah was afraid she'd crossed an OCD line that would preclude cooperation. She tapped her index finger on the desk as she said, "We need the report you sent to Mr. Howard. And we'd like it *now*, or we will be visiting another lawyer to see how else we can get the report. As heirs of this estate, we are entitled to see it."

At first, the thin woman didn't take her eyes off the smears on her desk. Slowly, she turned back to her computer and typed in a few more strokes. After a moment, she called her secretary to bring in the report from the printer. She spun around to get a tissue from the box on the bookcase and turned back.

Glaring at Hannah, she scrubbed away the smears as she said, "My records show Mrs. Time oversaw paying the taxes, not us. If they weren't paid, the neglect was hers, not ours."

A harried secretary rushed in and put a few papers on the desk before rushing out again. Ms. Bergman picked them up and straightened them before handing them to Hannah.

Essie took them with a slight nod of the head in thanks.

Hannah smiled, "I lied. We have the report from

the lawyer. If this report doesn't match that one, we'll have a big problem."

The upper lip of the accountant beaded in sweat. She took a sip from a water bottle, then dabbed her mouth and lip with a tissue. "You will find it matches the one with the lawyer. I run an honest business here."

"It better be honest." Hannah stood to go, and her sisters joined her as they went out the door. Once they got on the elevator, Hannah let out a big sigh. She looked at her sisters. "I was scared in there."

Sharon squeezed her arm. "Oh, but you looked in control of everything. I wouldn't want to mess with you."

"She typed so much I was afraid she was changing the report. That's why I challenged her. But at least now, we have the report."

"Don't bet on it," Essie said with a shake of her head. "She was lying."

"How do you know?" Sharon had her hand on her heart.

"Trust me," Essie told her. "She was lying. Her eyes gave her away. She did something to alter things. Or maybe she sent a message to someone. Something's going on here, and we need to find out what."

Chapter 20

Essie

The coffee table at the cottage was covered with papers. The sisters pored over them as the grandfather clock clicked away. They'd gone by the courthouse to check the property tax records and make sure the deed was recorded with their names on it.

A visit to the Better Business Bureau exposed many complaints against Assets, Inc. and their tie to Mr. Howard. If Ms. Bergman hadn't paid the taxes, it was at his direction. That meant he was out to take the cottage from them. Using the clock was the only way to find the answers in what they were supposed to do to keep it.

Essie sat back on the sofa and rubbed her sore neck and tired eyes.

Hannah, standing beside the coffee table, summed up the situation. "Girls, I can't see any other thing that's amiss. Mr. Howard did what Mother asked and put the deed in our names three years ago. At least he did that much right. But somehow, he persuaded Mother to let Assets, Inc. administer her money. They must have paid her bills and given her an allowance.

"But behind the scenes, Howie instructed Zoe Bergman to not pay the property taxes for the last several years, but didn't tell Mother. Once the deed was in our names, he probably told her we were taking care of it. Since we didn't get a bill for the taxes, we didn't know about any of it."

"So," Hannah began as she paced, "Howard told Mom the financial planners were taking care of it, and after Mom transferred the title to us, he told her we were taking care of it. Devious."

Essie noticed Hannah's hands were curled into fists as she paced. No doubt she wanted to hit something or someone.

Sitting a little further back on the sofa, Essie continued the summary, "But the county would have kept sending bills for the taxes, wouldn't they? How did Mother not see that and investigate?"

Hannah stopped and pounded a fist in her hand. "I don't understand it, but since we're dealing with two shady firms, it shouldn't be a surprise Mother didn't know."

Sharon yawned and said, "He must have lied to her. Or he changed the address for where the county sent the notices. He's seems to be an accomplished liar—I mean lawyer."

"Same difference," Hannah said as she sat in the overstuffed chair and leaned her head back against the side wings. Her eyes drooped until they closed. She didn't move, but a Mona-Lisa smile came across her face.

Essie smiled inwardly, sure she was visualizing what she'd like to do to Mr. Howard. An unsolicited yawn reminded her of her own fatigue. "It's been a while since we slept. Let's get some rest and afterward devise a plan to keep the cottage."

Without opening her eyes, Hannah mumbled, "Good idea."

Sharon got up from her place on the sofa. "Somehow we'll find a way to hold on to this place. But right now, I'm so tired I can hardly think straight."

Hannah yawned. "No worries. We'll come up with something. They underestimate the three of us. We deal with things most other people think are only imaginary."

Hannah opened one eye to look at Essie.

Essie smiled at the funny look and said, "They don't know who they're dealing with."

The clock was still ticking later when Essie got up before the others. She'd slept enough to feel refreshed.

She organized and straightened the papers on the coffee table. Financial stuff in one pile and property stuff in the other, both in chronological and alphabetical order. Done right the first time, it would be easy to find anything they might need.

Turning her attention to the videos strewn across the floor in front of the TV, she sat on a footstool and looked through the piles she'd started the day before. Or was it today? Or the day before that? Time was jumbled up now, she wasn't sure what day it was. When they stopped the grandfather clock later, they'd check their cell phones to find where in time they were.

She stacked the videos they'd watched and took them to the empty closet. Or at least she thought it was empty. In the back corner of the bottom shelf lay a single videotape cassette. How did she miss that one when she pulled them out? Very odd.

Putting the stack she'd brought in down in the opposite corner, she picked up the stray tape. It looked slightly different than the rest. A small red check mark was in one corner of the blank label.

Butterflies swirled in Essie's stomach as a prickly snake went up her spine, making her hair stand on end. She hurried into the living room and pushed the other videos aside. Ejecting the previous tape and pushing the new one in, she turned on the TV and sat on the sofa with the remotes. Her breath hardly came as she watched the out-of-nowhere videotape.

A picture came on, showing the living room she was sitting in. Her mother came from behind the camera to sit on the sofa where Essie sat. Essie looked at the seat cushion and ran her hand over it as she closed her eyes.

Her mother's voice came through the air to her. "Congratulations, girls! You've found my final video! I know you're not happy with me for making you watch those other tapes, but I had my reasons."

Essie hit the stop button. "Come quick! I found it!" she screamed from her seat. She ran down the hallway and pounded on the doors. "I've found Mother's last video!"

Chapter 21

Sharon

The smell of Sharon's coffee and cinnamon rolls filled the kitchen and made its way into the living room where Essie and Hannah were clearing the coffee table off. Wearing her new blue dress with red flowers, Sharon filled three mugs with coffee and took it into the living room on a tray.

Essie sat in the overstuff chair with her coffee mug. "Where did you get that dress? It's not red!"

Sharon smiled at her sister, but more so at Hannah who looked at her up and down with incredulous eyes. "I got it when we were shopping the other day. A special moment requires a special dress. Like it?" She spun around, making the skirt whirl around her still-white legs.

Quickly returning to the kitchen, she loaded another tray with plates and freshly zapped cinnamon rolls. Setting the tray down on the coffee table, she boasted, "I made the cinnamon rolls during one of my therapy sessions and reheated them this morning. Doesn't take but a few seconds to have a hot breakfast. Help yourself." She took her own mug of coffee and sat on the other end of the sofa, letting her sisters get the first rolls.

Hannah waved her coffee cup toward Essie. "Where did this stray video come from?" Hannah took a bite of the cinnamon roll. A look of sweet satisfaction spread across her face, and she quickly took another bite.

Essie finished chewing before speaking. "I woke up and came out here to clean. When I took the videos we'd watched back to the closet, it was there on the shelf in the back. I was sure I had taken all of them out of there, but I guess I missed one."

A shudder ran through Sharon, sending ripples into her coffee cup. "I told you this place is haunted. Someone must have put it there after you cleaned it out. It's not like you to miss one."

Hannah shook her head. "I told you it's not haunted. I can sense spirits, and there are none here."

"What if you can't sense Mom?" Sharon took another bite of her cinnamon roll so she wouldn't have to argue the point with Hannah.

Essie threw up her hands. "No matter, the tape's in the machine. Want to watch it?" She hit the button as they sat back with their plates of cinnamon rolls and mugs of coffee.

Their mother took her place on the sofa where Hannah and Sharon now sat. Her glowing smile was framed by her thick white hair. She wore what Sharon remembered her always wearing, capris and a button-down blouse.

With a lilt in her voice, their mother spoke to them. "Congratulations, girls! You've found my final video! I know you're not happy with me for making you watch those other tapes, but I had my reasons." She giggled slightly.

Sharon laughed along with her mother.

Their mother leaned back on the sofa and picked up a notebook. She looked at the camera, smiled, and waved the notebook around. "Don't want to forget anything," she said more to herself than to her daughters. She put on her reading glasses, scanned the list, and proceeded.

"I made this tape so I could tell you why things happened the way they did. Earlier this year, I was told I had terminal cancer and didn't have long to live. I'm spending my last days making sure things are ready for you. I put the cottage in your names several years ago. I didn't want to take any chances on who would inherit my home. Any remaining money can be split equally among you.

"Your father will be with me in my last hours and he will cremate my body and scatter my ashes in the ocean out front. It's where I want to be. I've always loved the ocean..." Her voice trailed off as she stared into space.

She blinked several times, as if coming out of a trance, and refocused her thoughts. "I didn't call you three with the news because I knew you'd rush here with your unresolved issues. I didn't want the stress of trying to keep you calm." Her face and her shoulders drooped.

Sharon's eyes filled with tears. Hearing sniffles around her, she passed the box of tissues around.

Their mother frowned. "I didn't want a funeral or gathering. If you can't be with me before I die, I don't want you here afterwards. I'm not trying to make you feel guilty. It's how I wanted it and since it's my time to die, I get to dictate how I will do it. No backtalk about it." Their mother sat quietly for a few moments.

Sharon blew her nose in the lull.

Their mother rubbed along her collarbone, a gesture Sharon had seen many times before when her mother was thinking about something serious. "After Hannah's wedding, I know none of you ever spoke to each other again. Your occasional phone calls made me see that somehow, some way I needed to reunite my family.

"We used to be a close family. I hope you saw that in the videos. I had you watch them because I wanted you to see how it used to be in hopes it could be that way again. I hope you will forgive each other. Your kids have lots of cousins they have never met. It's about time they did!" Their mother laughed as she gave her chest a love pat, as if touching all the love it felt.

"We lived a good life here in our cottage by the ocean. Your father stopped by to see you when he could. Your father is a good man! Don't you ever doubt it!" Leaning forward, she pointed at the camera as she said the words. "And he loves you three very much. Treat him with the respect he deserves."

Their mother sat back on the sofa and smiled. "Now girls, the most important reason why I need you to get along is so you can share this magical house. You have no idea what powers are inside here." She waved her arms around the room.

Sharon said aloud to her videoed mother, "We know about the clock."

Hannah shushed her.

Their mother lifted her eyebrows and gave them

a crooked smile. "If you followed my instructions, you've discovered the grandfather clock alters time inside the cottage when you set it to five o'clock. But that's not all it does."

She looked around her, making sure no one could hear her. She leaned toward the camera and whispered, "It's a portal. A portal to places and things you have no idea about."

The sisters looked at each other, each as equally surprised and confused as the others.

Their mother nodded. "Oh yes, there are lots of things you have not discovered yet, but more about that later."

She leaned back and continued. "You've likely discovered the cottage is at risk from taxes not being paid." She let out a big laugh. "If that crazy lawyer thinks he's found a way to take my cottage away from us, he's got another think coming. I know all about his antics. Don't worry, girls, I'm leaving money to pay the taxes."

Sharon heard Essie whisper a quiet "Thank you, Mother" as she let out a cry of relief.

Hannah looked happy too.

"I've been frugal. I think you'll find the practice has paid off. In the video closet, lift the bottom shelf and it will release a secret door. Behind that door is the money I've saved and cached there. I don't trust banks, you know. There's more than enough to pay the taxes owed on the cottage. Do that first. That'll starch Ol' Howie's shorts."

She smiled smugly. "Ol' Howie's a character isn't he." She broke out in a spirited laugh.

Growing serious again, she continued, "You can

split some of it equally between you, but most is intended for taxes and upkeep on the cottage. It's an investment in your future and in your children.

"Now about the clock. Your father gave me the clock when he built this cottage for me many years ago. It's a special grandfather clock. You three always fussed it never kept good time. That's because it doesn't keep time."

She gave them an all-knowing look. "It changes time inside the cottage. Many hours in the cottage are like a minute on the outside. Time is slowed only inside the cottage. It's a wondrous way to spend time with people you love. Your father and I spent a *lot* of years inside our cottage with the clock set to five…" She once again went into a memory-induced trance, but quickly blinked herself back to what she was saying.

"The clock has other functions your father can tell you about, but two of them I want you to know about now. If you set the clock to twelve and push the pendulum, it will call your father. He will walk out of the clock when he can manage to come. He's a busy man so he might not appear right away. Call him for a visit before you go home. He'd love to see you and has other things to tell you."

Their mother looked at her list and waved it slightly to fan her face. "The last clock function I will tell you about is a very special one. One that will also bless me."

She seemed tearful and took a moment to settle herself. "If each one of you will set the clock to three and push the pendulum, it will call me back for one last visit." She gave them a tearful smile. "I'll have twelve hours to spend with each of you until I must leave again...forever. Please use this time wisely." She wiped a falling tear away. "I can't wait to see you again!"

She glanced through her notebook and put it down. "I guess I've covered everything. Lastly, I want you girls to know you've been the joy of my life. I love you three very much and wish you all the good things of life.

"I hope you'll love the cottage as much as I have. You *must* keep it. It's a special place. The clock only works here and cannot be moved. Hang on to it! Pass this place along in your families. Please! I love you!" Their mother blew them a kiss before getting up to walk behind the camera and turn it off. Static filled the screen.

Essie hit the stop button and the static silenced. The ticking of the grandfather clock and quiet sobbing drifted through the living room.

Sharon picked up the tissue box, took several for herself, and passed the box on. She blew her nose. "Well," she said with tears in her voice, "I guess that settles that. We fight to keep the house. It's priceless."

Essie dried her eyes. "Agreed."

Still quietly sobbing into her tissue, Hannah nodded her head.

Pushing her tears aside, Sharon got up. "Let's find the money and go pay off the taxes. That'll get those vultures off our backs." She went to the closet and tugged on the bottom shelf. It shifted a little, and she tugged harder.

Hannah came up behind her. "Here, let me try."

Sharon moved to give Hannah room. Hannah tugged, wiggled, and shimmied the board until it gave way. Hannah backed away with it in her hands.

A small handle was flush with wall and only visible with the shelf removed. With Essie looking over their shoulders, Sharon and Hannah pulled on the handle until it gave way. A compartment looking like an old-time flour bin opened, revealing a rectangular tin box.

Sharon pulled out the box and wiggled its lid off. Inside were rubber-banded wads of money. Lots of them.

A collective gasp escaped the women.

She dropped the tin and it overturned, spilling wads of money that rolled across the floor and bumped into Essie's bare feet.

Sharon picked one up, pulled off the rubber band, and flipped through the $100 bills. Her mouth gaped in astonishment, mirroring her sister's expressions.

"Great gobs of tinsel!" Sharon said for the group. "We need to count this!"

Chapter 22

Hannah

Seeing the sky was sunny, Hannah stopped the clock. She might get to go home soon, but first, she needed to adjust her sleeping patterns back to normal.

The curtains were pulled tightly together before starting the money count. A bowl of water was set in the middle of the table for wetting fingers. The flipping of bills and whispered counting were the only sounds other than the rumble of the waves against the beach.

Their mother had rubber-banded ten $100 bills together, but they counted each one to make sure it was accurate. To help with the counting, they made piles of $10,000. In the end, they had forty-six piles of $10,000 scattered across the kitchen countertops and the table, plus a partial pile leftover. The sisters sat dazed amid the green.

Hannah spread ten $100 bills out like cards in her hands. She'd held that much before, but she'd had to work hard for it. "Where did Mother get this money? Even being frugal, how could she amass so much of it? I wonder if she had a job or something. I don't think Social Security pays this good."

Essie seemed dazed. Sharon waved her hand in front of her face, and Essie blinked back to life.

"Are you okay, Essie?" Hannah asked, smiling at her sister's money shock. "I guess you can remodel your kitchen now."

"I—I—don't know. Where did this come from? You don't think she robbed banks or anything, do you?"

Sharon clicked her tongue at the thought. "Of course not! She said she had lived frugally. I guess this is what happens when you do."

Essie held her head in her hands. "We're frugal too, but this? In a thousand years could we save this much! Where did it come from?"

Hannah sucked in a breath. "How old was Mother?" The wide eyes and shrugs of her sisters told her neither of them knew. "Could she have been over 100?"

Essie turned to look at the grandfather clock. "Who knows? With that thing altering time, she might have been 200 years old. That's something we'll have to ask Father when we call him."

Hannah moved to start picking up the piled money. "Let's get this put back and we'll do that—no! First, we need to go pay the taxes on this place before something happens. Let's put this away, but keep out enough to --"

A knock at the door sounded, sending a jolt of fear through Hannah.

"Yoo hoo! Anyone home?" A familiar, but grating voice sounded through the door.

Panic spread through the money-filled room like a wildfire across the prairie on a windy day. "Be quiet!"

Hannah whispered loudly. "She'll think we're not home and go away!"

Tiptoeing, she continued to pick up stacks of money and take them to the closet. Her sisters followed suit and helped gather the money to return to its hiding place, making several trips before it was tucked away. Several bundles fell from Essie's arms when she gathered more than she could carry.

The knocking and yelling at the door continued the whole time as they put the money away as quickly as possible. The door handle rattled several times as Elvira tried the door. Their visitor was rapping on the windows, likely while trying to peek in, while calling out her sickening yoo hoos.

The bin in the closet soon overran with jumbled bundles of money. They hid several of the bundles behind the few videos in the closet. After a mad flurry of activity, the bundles were shoved into the closet, and the door was secured.

Out of breath, the three sisters gathered in Hannah's bedroom as they waited for their unwanted guest to leave. The tapping and woo-hooing around the outside of the house continued for a while longer.

"Persistent old bitty, isn't she?" Hannah said with an eye roll as she paced around. "She's the one who told us about the delinquent taxes, which leads me to believe she's looking for any trick in the book to get a hold of this place. As soon as she's gone, let's go to the courthouse to settle."

Essie shook her head. "We can't walk in with nearly $20,000 in cash and say we're here to pay the taxes on our mother's house."

Sharon jumped in. "People might get suspicious.

We should get a money order or something."

Hannah stopped pacing. "Good idea, but can we get a money order for $20,000?"

"No," Essie said, "Money orders only go to a thousand dollars."

Hannah and Sharon stared at her with raised eyebrows.

Essie wave off their looks. "Trust me. I know what I'm talking about."

Hannah huffed. "We can't buy a bunch of thousand-dollar money orders or prepaid credit cards."

Sharon started breathing quickly. "How are we going to pay the taxes? With cash?"

Hannah shook her head. "Why not? We have it."

"No!" Essie said through gritted teeth. "It would bring down too much suspicion on us. Let's open a bank account and pay with a check."

Sharon's face lit up. "Great idea! I'm not afraid of banks."

Hannah shook her head. "We can't open a bank account. Banks have to report deposits of over $10,000 to the government." She explained as she saw the same question arise in their eyes. "They want to make sure we aren't laundering drug money or something like that."

Sharon started gasping again. "Oh dear, there goes our plan!"

Essie handed her a nearby paper bag to help with her breathing.

Hannah said in a whisper, "Let's keep it simple." Her sisters drew near. "We'll pay with cash." She raised her hand to stop Essie's argument before it began. "We'll tell them we went to the bank and withdrew the money. Or we should say we sold something. Either way, they have to take it."

Sharon put the paper bag away and said, "It makes sense. Keep it simple."

Essie looked away, shaking her head with her mental disagreement. She conceded, "I hope you're right."

A sense of relief came through Hannah and she felt her body relax. "Okay, it's settled. We pay in cash." She looked at the smiling face on Sharon and the still strained face of Essie.

Hannah held up a finger. "I don't hear any noises outside. I wonder if she's gone? Let's not make any noise until we know the ol' buzzard has flown off."

Hannah left to peer out each window. The driveway was clear and no other sign could be seen of Elvira. She gave the other two the thumbs-up signal.

Sharon got up off the bed. "We need to take along a copy of the deed showing it in our names. Where did we put that file?" She scurried off to the other room.

Essie looked at Hannah. "We should call the courthouse and find out exactly how much is owed. That way we'll know how much money to take."

Hannah couldn't help but grin. The always-practical Essie was sometimes more helpful than spur-of-the-moment Sharon. They complemented each other. She was the instigator. That's what she was. This called for action, and her sisters gave her ways to do it. They made a good team when they worked together.

When they reached the tax office at the courthouse, a tall woman at the counter slowly looked down her nose from one sister to the other as they huddled around the teller's station. Between them lay $18,500 in one-hundred-dollar bills on top of the deed to the cottage. "Where did you get this money?" she asked in the tone of a woman with her nose pinched by too-tight reading glasses.

Hannah cleared her throat. "I sold my car for cash and took money out of savings. Why?"

"Why did you bring it in cash?"

Hannah met the lady's stare with one of her own. "I don't trust banks. I only do business in cash."

Sharon stepped in. "We want to pay our taxes with cash. Is there something wrong with that?"

The woman glared at Sharon. "It's unusual for this amount of cash to be brought in. Haven't you ever heard of a cashier's check?"

Essie slapped the top of the counter, causing the woman behind it to jump. "She told you why we brought cash. Is there something wrong with our money, or do we need to go see the mayor or governor or someone like that?"

The woman glared at her. "Since it's a large sum of cash, I'll have to check with my manager." She locked the money drawer and left.

Hannah took a deep breath and whispered, "Thanks, you two. I didn't know it would be so hard. I don't normally lie, but in this case, it's necessary. Don't put me on the naughty list, Sharon."

Sharon chuckled. "Don't worry. I won't. But this is nerve-wracking! At the same time, it's invigorating! I haven't had such an exciting time since I don't know when." She giggled, holding her hand over her mouth and nose to help her breathe slower.

The nasal-voiced woman came back, followed by a short balding man who looked as pinched-nosed as she did. "How may we help you?" he asked the sisters in the same nasal tone.

Hannah fought to hide a grin from the twin snobs. "We want to pay the back taxes on our property with cash." She pushed the huge pile of bills slightly to draw his attention. "Miss—" she waved her hand at the unfriendly woman, "whoever won't take our money. It's all here. Count it if you don't believe me. I think you'll find you owe us change."

The man squinted at Hannah with a look of distrust while he picked up the bills. Looking down, he flipped through them quickly, using his rubber thumb to count the bills individually.

With each thousand dollars, he stacked them and pushed them toward the woman who ran a yellow marker over the bills. The man continued to count and ended with the amount indicated by Hannah. The woman muttered the results of her yellow marker indicating the bills were legal tender.

"Okay, Ms. —" the man paused.

"Headless. Hannah Headless."

A puzzled look spread across his face, but disappeared as quickly as it came. "How good of you to finally pay your taxes, Ms. Headless. We owe you $15.41." He typed furiously into the computer.

Sharon took her hand away from her face. "Will our taxes be up-to-date starting today?"

The man eyed the three women through narrowed eyes, like he was trying to read their minds. "Technically, yes. Why?"

Hannah felt a surge of ire run through her. She

tapped the countertop with her finger as she said, "None of your business. Make sure it shows paid. Plus, we want to change the address where the notices are sent. We are changing accounting firms."

The man didn't take his eyes off Hannah who found it easy to return his steely glare. He didn't intimidate her. If it hadn't been for Essie tugging at her shirt, she'd have broken something. Either the pen with the flower taped on the end or him. Her hands hurt from her fingernails stuck into her palms.

With an aloof toss of his head, he walked away, pulling the teller along with him.

Hannah couldn't tell if he was going to give them their change or call the police.

After a few minutes of nervous shuffling, the sisters saw the woman come back with address-change forms for Hannah to sign. Returning as she finished signing the last form, the snobby man brought her a receipt. He tossed it down in front of the teller and walked away without saying a word.

Picking up the receipt, Hannah saw it showed all taxes and penalties had been paid. As they left the building, the three sisters breathed a sigh of relief.

Hannah let out a whoop. "The weight of the world is off my shoulders! The cottage is ours!" She did a little dance on the sidewalk.

Sharon joined her in doing a little jig while Essie looked on.

Hannah stopped the celebrating. "But we're not done. We have to plan on how to get rid of the buzzards for good!"

Chapter 23

Essie

For the first time since she'd arrived, Essie felt relaxed. She sat on the sofa with her feet on the coffee table, letting the day's tensions flow out of her. Beside her, Sharon did the same thing, with a bowl of popcorn by her side. Hannah sat sideways in the overstuffed chair like she had as a teenager. Essie felt a twinge of envy at her lithe sister.

On the coffee table lay the paper showing the tax bill paid in full. Their cottage was safe from the vultures circling it. The grandfather clock, set to twelve o'clock, ticked off the seconds of relaxation. The sound of Sharon's munching slowly died away, and the three sisters dozed off.

The peace was shattered by the sound of the doorbell ringing several times. They were shaken from their slumber.

Hannah rubbed her eyes. "I guess twelve o'clock doesn't alter time."

"Too bad," Essie said as she got up from the sofa. "I needed more of a nap." She went to the window and peeked out between the edges of the curtain. She let out a moan. "It's our nemeses. Howie, Ed, and Elvira. Heaven help us!"

The pounding on the door conveyed the impatience of their visitors. Mr. Howard bellowed, "We know you're in there! We need to talk to you!"

Anger roared through Essie like a flood. This place was theirs. They didn't have to endure this rude behavior.

"Sisters, this is our cottage. Those trespassers have no business here." She went to the door and grabbed the handle. Behind her, Sharon and Hannah stood firm.

Flinging the door open, the three sisters walked out onto the front porch, forcing their unwanted guests to take a step backward. Hannah slammed the door shut behind them.

With crossed arms and wide stances, the trio blocked the door.

"What do you want?" Essie asked in a voice the same temperature as Arctic permafrost.

Elvira's face beamed from underneath her makeup. "Oh, you are here! I—I mean we have a proposal for you to consider. A very profitable proposal, I might add. Trust me, you'll love it! Hear us out."

She waved at Ed to come forward. He stumbled as he stepped up and put his thumbs behind his suspenders.

"The three of us have joined ranks and decided to make you an offer you can't refuse." He stretched out his suspenders as he looked at his partners with a grin. "We are prepared to offer you not half a million dollars...not three-quarters of a million dollars...but one *million* dollars for your cottage and the acreage with it."

He rocked back and forth on his heels, with a perfect what-do-ya-think-about-that grin on his face as he nodded.

Essie tapped her foot. "I guess you found out we paid the property taxes on this place, huh? Foiled your plan for getting it cheap?"

Elvira stepped forward, pushing past the still inflated Ed whose thumbs continued to slide up and down his suspenders. "Now, I think you got the wrong impression about me offering to pay those for you. I was trying to help you out of a tough spot. But apparently," she let out a giggle, "you didn't need help. My mistake. But now, we're here making you a fair and honest offer."

Essie looked at her two sisters who mirrored her poker-face stare. "No thanks. The place is not for sale for any amount of money. Good day." She turned to go, but the protests of the three partners held her back.

Elvira dropped her massive purse and stepped forward, her hands twined together in a prayerful pose. "But—but that's a fair offer! And I doubt anyone else would offer you that much for this old rundown cottage." She waved her hands at the house. "You need to think about our offer. You stand to make a ton of money off this place here and now!"

"How many times must we say it? It's not for sale!" Hannah leaned forward. "Now go away and leave us alone!"

Sharon pointed a finger at them from behind Essie. "Trespassing! That's what you're doing! We should call the police!"

Mr. Howard stretched out to his full height like a grizzly cornering its prey. "You don't understand. We want this place, and we're willing to pay for it. Think about this offer and take it."

The door opened behind the sisters. Quickly turning, they saw a tall, bearded, distinguished-looking man dressed in a three-piece suit step outside and pull the door shut behind him. Essie felt her body relax. Their father was here! He'd back them up in fending off this ugly partnership.

Father Time stepped in front of his daughters. "I think you heard my daughters correctly the first time," their father said in a deep voice that carried the authority of timelessness. "I suggest you heed their answer to your offer. This place is not for sale and never will be in your lifetimes."

Ed stepped off the porch. "Mr. Time, if we could prevail upon you to consider our offer. We could raise it a little if you prefer."

Their father spoke over his shoulder, "Sharon, go call the police and report trespassers who refuse to leave." Obeying her father's direction, Sharon scurried into the house.

"Come on, Howie," Elvira said, tugging on his suit coat. "It's no use." She joined Ed who followed her down the sidewalk toward the driveway.

Mr. Howard stood, planted firmly on the top step of the porch, hands on hips, glaring at their father with contempt. Stabbing the air with his finger, he growled, "You have no title to this cottage! My offer extends to the owners of this property, not you." Catching himself before he went too far, he paused and regained control of himself. "Wait a minute here. If you'd let me explain—"

Their father stood taller and took one step forward. "Time," he roared, "waits for no one!"

Mr. Howard cowered as he backed down the steps.

Their father took another step forward. "Your time, however, has run out. You leave my girls alone, or you'll regret it."

Elvira called out as she and Ed got in the car. "Howie, give it up!"

Mr. Howard stood for another moment before backing away. "I'm not through here." He spun around and stomped his way to the driver's seat. He sent a shower of gravel toward the house as he sped away.

"Oh Father!" Sharon exclaimed when the others came inside. She rushed to him and embraced him around his waist.

He spread his arms wide, inviting Essie and Hannah in. They joined their sister in their father's arms.

He gave them a bear hug. "Soooo good to hold my girls again!" He gave each one of them a peck on the forehead before letting them go. "Essie, set the clock to five so we have more time together."

As Essie set the clock, Sharon led him by the hand to the overstuffed chair. She rushed off to the kitchen, reappearing soon with a platter full of cookies and a pitcher of milk to set on the coffee table. In a minute, she rushed back with glasses and napkins.

"Sharon, you were always the perfect little hostess," their father said with a chuckle in his voice. "Look at this! In an instant, you make your visitors feel welcome."

Sharon smiled as she poured milk for the four of them. "It's what I love to do, Father." She sat on the sofa alongside her two sisters.

Essie took a small bite off a cookie. "What about Hannah and me? What have we been?"

Holding a cookie in one hand and a glass of milk in the other, their father sat back in the overstuffed chair. His smiling eyes swept over his girls as he took a drink of milk before setting it back on the coffee table. He loosened the buttons on his vest.

"Essie, you've been the leader. You like to do things by the book. And you, Hannah, wanted to do things your own way. I can see you still do. By the way, you look good in black. Don't let your sisters tell you otherwise."

Hannah let out a laugh that sounded like a cry of triumph. "Thanks, Father."

Essie didn't want to talk about wardrobes or how they'd turned out. Until the business with Mr. Howard and the others was done, she was stuck here. She wanted to know how to get home.

Finishing her cookie, she took the conversation back to where she wanted it. "Father, we're in a bind over this house. Those people want this house and want it badly, enough to do unethical things to get it. Did you know the property taxes weren't paid on this place for the last three years? That Howard man was going to buy it out from under us by paying the back taxes."

Her father nodded and ate the last of his cookie. He sat back in the chair and folded his hands together. The grandfather clock provided the background tempo for thought. "I knew. So did your mother. She knew

Howard was conning people out of their houses and money by using loopholes in the law. She decided to try to 'bring him down,' to use her words. She created the situation so you girls would have to work together to solve it."

Hannah let out a slight laugh. "We'd guessed as much. Making us watch those videos."

Essie felt heat rise from her neck to her face. Their mother set them up. She knew it, but hearing her father say it made it more concrete. She rubbed her temples to ease the pain of being manipulated more than she ever thought possible.

"Now, now, Essie," her father said, "don't get your bloomers in a knot. It's your mother's way of trying to get you girls back together. She was desperate and this way, she would have the utmost pleasure of achieving two of her goals."

As sophisticated as he looked, seeing her father with a slight milk mustache made Hannah muse, "Killing two birds with one stone, eh?"

Her father got a look of amusement on his face. "That's cliché, darling."

Frustrated, she let out groan. She didn't have time for this sweet talk. Her sisters might dismiss their mother's plan, but she was angry with her mother for doing it and perturbed with herself for falling for it. Resisting the urge to pull on her hair, she gritted her teeth so hard her jaw hurt.

A nudge in the ribs from Sharon took Essie out of her thoughts.

"Chill, sis!" Sharon said as she took another cookie. "You were set up by the best."

Hannah leaned forward to see Essie around

Sharon. "What are you upset about, Essie? Because you had to get along with Sharon and me for a little while?"

Essie felt her face get hot again. Both sisters and her father were grinning at her, like she'd been caught in a bad practical joke. With a roll of her eyes, she released the anger and tension. She had to admit it. Her mother's plan had worked.

Throwing her hands up in surrender, she asked, "What do we do to get rid of our three nemeses?"

With a Cheshire cat grin, her father leaned forward. "Your mother planned that too. Sharon, Santa's sleigh works year-round, doesn't it?"

She nodded.

"Can he pick up Easter and the kids and Headless and the boys and bring them all here?"

She nodded again.

"Have him do it."

Chapter 24

Sharon

Under the sliver crescent of the moon high in the dark sky, the cottage's kitchen was the center of activity as Sharon directed the cooking for the guests due to arrive any minute. Sharon stirred another batch of cookies while the two cakes baked in the oven.

Hannah was working on the large roast in an electric cooker, putting potatoes, onions, mushrooms, carrots, and celery around it, her family's favorite dish. To the side, Essie was slicing a mountain of vegetables into snack-size lengths. She'd told Sharon her tribe loved to eat all the time and having lots of nutritious snacks on hand was important.

The living room was quiet, nine-fifteen showing on the face of the clock. Their father had gone back to wherever he usually stayed. One day, she'd ask him where that was and exactly what he did there.

A knock at the door paralyzed the activity in the kitchen. Tiptoeing to the front window, Sharon parted the curtain enough to allow one eye to barely see the front porch.

There stood a large man in red shorts and a red

tank top and a taller man dressed in black. A cry of joy
brought the other sisters running to the front door as
Sharon threw it open.

"Ho ho ho, Sharon dear!" Santa reached out and
pulled his wife close. "I've missed you!" he whispered
in her ear.

Sam stood behind his father. "Mom!" he cried
out as he hugged Sharon.

Holding him close, Sharon whispered, "What
about your classes?"

Sam pushed her back and said, "Dad said he'd
get me back there before morning. They'll never know I
was gone."

Sharon looked around at the crowded cottage.

Hannah jumped into the arms of the tall man
behind Santa, nearly knocking his head off, but she
steadied it before it fell. Her sons gathered around her.

The sound of swarms of children drifted in from
the beach in front of their house. Essie took off at a jog
to join them.

Sharon pulled Santa inside. "Did the elves come
with you?"

He shook his head as he followed her into the
kitchen to check on the cakes. "No, they decided to stay
and keep the factory running. Time is running out and
there's no time for vacations. I should have stayed, but
you needed me worse."

The cake tops sprang back under her gentle
touch. She pulled them out of the oven and slid two
pans of cookies in. "I hope this plan doesn't take too
long to work itself out. What did you do with the
sleigh?"

"It's out front."

Sharon wiped her hands on her apron. "We set up tents on the side of the house to hide it from view. The reindeer can stay in there too. We had the feed store deliver hay for them."

Santa gave her a kiss on her rosy cheek before leaving to move things to the tent. Sam followed behind to help him.

Hannah and Headless came into the kitchen, holding hands and whispering to each other.

She thought about how they made a nice couple. Headless had a handsome face. Too bad about his head though. She wondered if he'd ever forgotten where he put it. She felt her face redden when she realized she was staring. Spinning around, she busied herself with frosting the fresh cake.

Something lightly touched her from behind before the loud "Boo!" Sharon jumped. The icing-laden spatula flew. Quickly spinning around, she saw four small eyes smiling up at her.

"Are you our Aunt Sharon?" asked one of the two identical children, blinking at her in wonderment. "Do you make the toys we get at Christmas?"

Her pounding heart settled down as she looked at her nephews, with their blonde curly hair and brown eyes staring at her like she was a three-headed cat. From their appearance, they were Essie's boys.

She smiled at them and said, "I help make toys, but our elves and your Uncle Santa are the ones who make most of them. What are your names?"

One of the boys slapped his chest. "I'm Alan and—" he slapped the chest of his sibling, knocking him back a step— "this is my brother Ned."

Ned rubbed his chest while scowling.

She got two spoons out of the drawer and dipped them in the frosting, offering Ned the first spoon as a reward for taking a hit from his brother. "Nice to meet you, Ned and Alan. My job at the workshop is cooking for Santa and the elves. Do you like my cake frosting?"

The boys put the whole sample into their mouths. With beaming smiles, the twins gave their approval.

Sharon put her finger to her lips. "Don't tell anyone I let you have a taste of my frosting, or else everyone will want one and I won't have enough frosting to put on the cakes."

With the spoons licked clean, the twins gave them back to her before scampering off, allowing Sharon to finish frosting the two cakes.

The last pan of cookies was in the final minutes of baking when a solitary child walked in. Dressed in dark clothes, with dark hair, and a dark attitude about him, there was little doubt about whose son he was.

Sharon looked at him and said, "Which one of my nephews are you? Horace or Huntley?"

The boy's eyes widened in surprise that she knew his name. "I'm Huntley." He stared at her with narrowed eyes. "Who are you?"

Sharon felt the boy's thinly disguised distaste, but didn't know why he felt that way. He didn't know her or the love she felt for her unknown nieces and nephews. She put her hands on her hips, determined to battle for his affection. She'd kill him with kindness if she had to. "I'm your Aunt Sharon. I live at the North Pole."

Huntley ran his finger along the countertop,

stealing glances at the cookies while trying not to show it. "Oh yeah, the one who makes Christmas toys for us? You live in the cold and ice and snow?"

Sharon pushed a cookie toward him. He looked at her with dark, questioning eyes. She nodded and he took the cookie and bit into it. His features softened as he ate.

Sharon felt sure she'd made a small victory in this battle. "Yes, I love the cold. The heat here in Florida has bothered me since I got here, but I'm making the best of it."

She put her finger to her lips. "Don't tell anyone I let you eat a cookie. Otherwise, they'll all be in here wanting one and I won't have any for later. You're an extra special boy because you get to try them ahead of time."

Huntley looked out the side of his narrowed eyes as he finished his cookie. Sharon knew he'd be a hard one to convince she was on his side, but she saw it as a challenge and smiled slightly at the object of her determination.

Gathering everyone into the tents by the beach for a late-night snack proved to be harder than Sharon expected. Essie's children were everywhere, but seldom all in the same place.

Used to dealing with crowds of eaters, Sharon knew how best to gather them in one place. She marched out of the cottage holding a large decorated cake. Like the Pied Piper, children followed her to the beach and inside the tent.

Easter stepped to one end of the tables covered with sandwich makings, cookies, and cakes. "Quiet please!   Children, sit down and behave!   Family meeting time! We have things we need to discuss."

The children ignored her until Sam stepped forward and gave a short, shrill whistle. Easter thanked him and motioned for his family to sit.

Setting a large plate of vegetables on the table, Sharon stood aside as her fifteen nieces and nephews took their seats. When Huntley and Horace sat at another table apart from their cousins, Sharon's heart winced with anxiety at seeing how the two dark-haired boys were mostly ignored by their light-haired cousins. Sam made his way over to them, relieving her distress a little.

Sharon waved at her sisters to join her at the head of the table.

The din of voices calmed to a whispering level as everyone ate. Essie explained their plan. "Ever since we arrived, we've been plagued by three people who are determined to take our mother's property from us. The cottage and the land around it belongs to the family, and we are determined to keep it."

She lowered her voice, because she had everyone's attention, and because she wanted to keep her voice from carrying too far beyond the reach of the tent. "Easter, Pete, and Marcia will go outside to watch the perimeter of the place to make sure we're not being spied on. We don't want anyone watching what's going on around here."

Sharon's heart skipped a beat. She hadn't thought of it, but now that Essie mentioned it, Mr. Howard's determination to get their cottage would push him to do such a thing. If he learned of their plan, he would stop at nothing to wrest this place away from them. She wiped her upper lip with a napkin, glad

Essie had thought to send out scouts to make sure their plans were unheard.

Hannah moved to the side of the table. She called her sons and Sam over to the big table. Her voice was low as she explained more. "Mother and Father devised a plan to scare the pants off that Mr. Howard and his accomplices. We want them to think this house is haunted and possessed. If they do, they'll run out of here, never to return. But we also want to make it so outlandish no one will believe their story. We'll need everyone's help with this. Will you help us?"

A boisterous yell rang through the tent. Sharon saw Horace and Huntley smiling as they nodded in agreement. That made her heart lift. Working together with their cousins might get them on speaking terms.

Essie waved her hands in the air, trying to restore order. "Settle down, kids! We need to make assignments."

Sam gave another loud whistle and quiet followed.

Essie walked to the middle of the table beside Hannah and leaned in, whispering, "But first, let me tell you about a few things. A few things that might frighten you."

She turned to look at Hannah. "You should tell them since it's your idea."

Sharon was barely able to stay calm. Hannah's idea was the best thing ever. To bring their mother back while their families were here. Their mother would love to see her grandchildren. Plus, she could apologize to her mother for not coming to visit more often.

Hannah explained how they planned to set the clock, and their mother would appear. While her sons seemed unruffled, Essie's children seemed frightened, but she assured them they were safe. Easter told them he would be close by and wouldn't let anything happen to them.

Santa and Sam seemed skeptical of the idea. Sharon told them to keep an open mind and see what happened. There was more magic around than they realized.

In the dark of night, a line of people made their way from the tent to the cottage. Twenty-two people crowded into the small living room and faced the clock. The children huddled close to their parents with eyes wide and fear etched on their faces. Except for Huntley and Horace who looked bored with the hubbub.

Sharon set the grandfather clock to three as her sisters stood on either side of her. Behind them, stood their children and husbands waiting, shifting from foot to foot, mussing with their clothing, and childish whispering asking what was going to happen. The rustling of impatience blended in with the ticking clock.

The pendulum swung back and forth in a hypnotizing rhythm. The seconds ticked louder and louder, increasing each time until finally the little children stuck their fingers in their ears.

A reflection formed in the glass of the pendulum case, faint at first, but growing clearer with the ticking. Sharon rubbed her eyes as the reflection seemed to move out of the clock and a faint shadowy figure stood in front of it. More ticks. The figure became clearer. A few more ticks and their mother stood there, smiling at her clan.

Chapter 25

Hannah

Words couldn't form in Hannah's throat. It was dry and frozen in amazement. Her mother stood in front of the grandfather clock, looking like she had the last time she'd seen her. Her gray hair was neatly done, styled around her head like a halo. She wore her favorite sundress and held her faded sunhat in her hands. She opened her arms and said, "My girls!"

Hannah's mind still didn't believe what it was looking at and failed to send the command to her feet to move forward.

Sharon rushed straight to her mother's arms, jolting Hannah out of her stupor. She followed Essie into her mother's embrace. Her mother's arms were cold, like they'd been in front of an air conditioner too long, but the warmth of the hug and kisses from her mother warmed her insides.

A sob bubbled out of Hannah's throat. "Mother, you're here!"

Her mother pulled back from them. "What a treat to see you all here at the same time! Who summoned me?"

Sharon meekly held up her hand.

Giving a sweet smile, her mother said, "I will spend much of my time with you, Sharon. How nice of you to share our time with all these people, but you've always been the kindest of my girls." She gave Sharon an extra hug. "Now introduce me to this crowd!"

The sisters turned to see their families assembled in the living room. Hannah saw a faint smile on the face of Headless, an expression she seldom saw there in the presence of others. He had a hand on the shoulders of their sons. She waved them over.

No fear was in her sons' eyes. Meeting their dead grandmother was not shocking to them since they normally hung out with ghosts and ghoul friends. Horace had a crooked grin on his face.

Her mother embraced Headless warmly. "Good to see you again, son," she said with a voice of welcome. "And are these fine-looking boys Horace and Huntley? Oh my, how tall you've grown! I bet you'll be taller than your dad someday."

Huntley looked up at his dad with an I-can't-wait smile.

Her mother embraced Horace. "How old are you?"

Horace mumbled in his conjured deep voice, "Ten and a half."

"Ten and a half—going on sixteen. What a handsome young man you are. You're going to break hearts!"

Horace gave her a crooked smile. He pushed Huntley forward when he moved back.

Huntley was smothered by his grandmother's kisses. He resisted her cuddles as best as he could, but his grandmother was very persistent.

She leaned over to look him square in the eyes. "That must make you seven years old, Huntley. You're not my cuddly little ghoul anymore."

"No, ma'am, I'm grown up." Huntley wiped his face on his sleeve. Hannah frowned at him, but he looked away before making eye contact.

Hannah gathered her family and moved to the side to allow Sharon, Santa, and Sam to greet her mother.

As they moved past Essie's family, Hannah saw the wide, scared eyes of the Bunny children staring at their grandmother who had appeared out of the clock like magic. She pulled on the arms of her sons and pointed to the frozen group.

The three of them walked in front of the spellbound group. Breaking their line of vision brought them out of their stunned stares. "It's okay," Hannah said to Essie's children. "There's nothing to fear."

Horace stuck to his cool pose, with hands stuck in his pockets. "She's mostly a regular person." His hand flicked to accentuate the important words. "Because she's been dead a little while doesn't mean she's not real. She still loves us. We're her grandkids. Besides, if my chicken brother here isn't afraid of her, you shouldn't be either."

Huntley's face turned red. "I ain't a chicken!"

A big grin spread across Horace's face as he reached out and tousled his brother's dark hair.

Marcia had Ned, Alan, and Sarah hanging on around her waist. Marcia looked as scared as her younger siblings, but managed to utter, "But it's so—so—so weird!"

Horace went to stand by Marcia who was his elder by three years. He leaned close to her and whispered, "That's what makes this so cool. Who else in this big world can say they got a hug from their dead grandmother? Come on, I'll go with you."

Horace pulled on her arm as Huntley stepped forward and waved for their cousins to follow. With baby steps and fearful looks, the bunch shuffled their way closer to their grandmother who smiled at the uneasy procession in her direction. They made their way to Essie and Easter and stood behind them, using their parents for a shield in case they didn't like what they saw.

When Horace came back, Hannah gave him a shoulder hug for his efforts with his cousins. They watched together as Grandmother Time didn't push herself on the Bunny clan, but spoke to them as they stood behind their parents.

The greetings and hugs were interrupted by a cell phone ring. The noise immediately stopped as Hannah pulled out her phone and answered. "Mr. Howard? Yes, we are home tonight. We'll be up for a while yet."

Pause. "We told you we didn't want to sell."

Pause. "Okay, okay. Come by with your final offer. See you in a bit." She ended the call and smiled. "He took the bait!"

"Places everyone!" Essie's rally cry sent people scurrying off to set their plan in motion.

An hour later, the three sisters sat on the sofa, sipping tea, enjoying cookies, and talking of the fun times they'd had in the house. On the TV, a video showed them as girls hunting Easter eggs on the porch and in the yard of the little house.

The doorbell rang through the mostly empty cottage. The three sisters couldn't help but break out into laughter before shushing each other to be serious.

"Come in!" sang out Hannah in her sweetest voice.

The door slowly opened, revealing Mr. Howard in a three-piece suit with his briefcase. Behind him stood Elvira, in her sequined and overly taut in her sundress, and Ed in his brown suit, thumbs in his blue suspenders. None of the sisters rose to invite them in, but sat there looking at them, with their sweetest smiles on.

Howie hesitated a moment before stepping in. "Good evening, ladies. Nice to see you again." He came toward the sofa, but the coffee table was pulled close enough he couldn't get around it to shake their hands.

Essie waved toward the overstuffed chair.

He sat on the edge of the seat. Elvira and Ed sat in the two dining room chairs pulled into the living room for the occasion.

Without taking her eyes off the TV screen, Sharon told him, "We're watching videos of living in the cottage, and the fun times we've had here."

Mr. Howard glanced at the TV, then rubbed his hands together. He cleared his throat and said, "What's going on here? Why are you acting strangely?"

Hannah looked at him, as wide-eyed and innocent as she could fake. "Strange? We're acting strange?" Seeing him nod, she waited until she saw tiny beads of sweat appear on his forehead. "We're a strange family. Isn't that right, sisters?"

"Yes," Essie answered. "We're an odd bunch."

Sharon nodded her consensus.

Mr. Howard's face reddened as he snapped open his briefcase. "I don't have time for games. I have paperwork here ready for your signature. My final offer is to buy only the land around the cottage. You may keep the cottage, the yard, and the land from it to the beach. That equals about one and a half acres. The rest of the land will be sold to me for one million dollars."

He waited for a reaction.

The sisters kept staring at the TV. The sound of videoed childhood laughter filled the room.

"I don't have all night. Yes or no, ladies."

Hannah let out a big sigh. "What do you think, Mother?"

From the hallway, their mother came into the room and stood beside the sofa. "My land is not for sale. Neither is my cottage. All of it belongs to my daughters and their families."

A smile slowly spread across her face as a look of horror spread across Mr. Howard's. Elvira and Ed knocked over their chairs as they sprang up and ran toward the front door. With his hand poised on the door knob, Ed turned to watch the scene play out as Elvira tried to hide behind him.

Mr. Howard jumped up from the chair, knocking his briefcase and papers all over the floor. His eyes were wide and his large mouth was gaping as hoarse, high-pitched shrieks came out. He backed until he hit the wall between the living room and dining room. Spread-eagled against the wall, he choked out, "What — what — you — dead — dead! How — how —"

Their mother took a step toward him.

He closed his eyes and tried to melt into the wall.

Stopping, she gave him a sideways look. "I'm supposed to be dead, you say? I am! I died several months ago. And while I'm dead, I hear you and that crooked accounting firm of yours didn't pay my property taxes with the money I gave you. What did you do with my money, Howie?" She took another step forward.

The man's face contorted into a silent scream as tears and sweat fell together on his starched white shirt.

The sound of a horrified scream came from Elvira right before her eyes rolled back in her head. She fell to the floor, knocking Ed off his feet. The heap of the two people in front of the door, Elvira out cold and Ed with his face in the crook of his arm while he whimpered, prevented Mr. Howard's escape.

Looking from the door to his friends, a bug-eyed, I'm-trapped look spread across his face as he looked back at their mother.

Their mother walked up to him and poked him in his large stomach. "Howie, did you want my place so badly you'd steal it from my girls? This place is worth millions! Don't be greedy."

He shut his eyes tightly, but barely opened one of his eyes to look at their mother. He quickly closed it again. "I didn't mean to," he squeaked.

Biting her tongue, Hannah kept silent despite wanting to yell out something sarcastic. She watched Essie's knuckles go white as she tightened her fists. A look of amused pity was on Sharon's face, her hand over her mouth to keep her smile from spreading.

Turning to look at her girls on the sofa, their mother gave them a wink before turning her attention back to the sobbing Mr. Howard. "Did you steal money from me?"

"Nnnnooooo!"

She poked him in the stomach again. "Don't lie to me! Do you know where liars go after they die? I haven't been there, but I've heard about the heat of it."

"Nnnnoooooo! I mean, okay, I took some of your money, but Zoe took most of it. Go haunt her instead of me!" He sobbed loudly. "Please, God, help me out of this!"

Their mother leaned up close to his face, using all her five-foot-four stature to get as close to his face as she could. "You want out of this, Howie? Change your ways. Repay what you've stolen. Learn what the word 'no' means. Learn to be an honorable lawyer and not a greedy jerk."

She turned and started to walk away, but stopped. "Oh, and do some pro bono work occasionally. You'll make points with the Big Guy upstairs. You're in negative numbers right now. You need to do extra credit."

Mr. Howard relaxed slightly, lowering his arms. He inched his way toward the door. "Yes, ma'am. I'll do better in the future."

Walking to the coffee table, she pushed his briefcase and the scattered papers away from her. "This place is not for sale. Not in pieces. Nor as a whole. Quit bothering my family about it. And take your two dogs with you."

She pointed at the two people blocking the door and the mess of his briefcase. "Pick up your stuff and get out of here. Don't ever darken my door again, or I'll come back and haunt you to your dying day!" She walked over to him again and stuck her cold finger in his face on the last two words to make her point. "You understand me?"

"Y—Y—Yes, ma'am. Yes, ma'am." The man nodded his head so violently Hannah wondered if it would fly across the room.

Mr. Howard bent over the still whimpering Ed to pull his arm away from his face. After several attempts, Ed opened his eyes enough to see who was tugging on him. Mr. Howard told him to get out and take Elvira with him.

Ed grabbed the lapels of Mr. Howard's suit coat and pulled. "This place is haunted! Get me outta here!"

Mr. Howard yanked his coat free of Ed's hands and pointed at the moaning Elvira. "Help me get the whale out of here. She's blocking the door."

Together they jerked on the large arms which evoked a moan out of Elvira. Blinking her eyes and coughing, she yelled, "Where am I?" She flailed her arms around, trying to rise.

Ed pulled on her arm to urge her to get up. "You're in a haunted house, and you're blocking the door. Get out of my way!"

He pushed her as she was getting to her feet, knocking her down again, but away from the door. Grabbing the door knob, he flung the door open and ran out...straight into Headless who stood in the doorway. The impact pushed Headless back a step. His head fell from its cradle. He caught it mid-air. Turning his head so that it was facing out, Headless put it in the crook of his arm.

Hannah smiled to herself. Headless was right on time. And his timing couldn't have been any better.

Chapter 26

Essie

Still sitting on the sofa, Essie watched her mother welcome her son-in-law into the cottage. "Oh Headless, how good of you to drop by. And I see you brought friends with you!" Their mother stood back to allow Headless to walk in the door.

The ghosts of two pirates floated through the wall next to the door to stand beside Headless in the entryway. The one wearing the tricorn hat took it off and bowed to their mother.

"Good evening, Francis," the head said. "Nice to see you again. I hope I'm not intruding."

"Of course not," her mother said. "The real intruders were just leaving, weren't you three?"

Ed shot out the door like he was a cannonball fired from a cannon.

Letting out the most hair-raising screams of fright, Elvira found her feet and sidled past Headless before running after Ed.

Mr. Howard, still on his hands and knees as he gathered his papers and briefcase, looked up. The silent-scream grimace came across his face again, but no sound came out. His eyes were so wide Essie thought they might pop out of his head.

Headless held his arm out to his two companions. "May I introduce my friends, Peg-Leg Brown and Rummy Jones. They came to see your place. They might be able to patrol the grounds after we leave."

Their mother waved her arm toward the center of the room. "Any friends of yours are friends of mine. Come on in, boys!"

Headless walked over and towered above Mr. Howard whose grimace included tears coming down his face and murmured prayers.

Rummy Jones floated over and knelt beside him. "Wha' ya doin' down 'ere?"

Essie's heart gave a start when she watched Mr. Howard's face contort more. Maybe they'd gone too far. What if it froze that way?

Jumping up, Mr. Howard sidled his way past Headless and the ghost. He backed away from them and bumped into Santa who stood in the doorway. Turning, his distorted face eased a little back into a normal shape. A funny half-grin, half-grimace came out of the transformation.

"Ho ho ho! What do we have here?" Santa stood stroking his long white beard and laughing as he surveyed the scene. "Why, Headless, my friend, how nice to see you again! I didn't know you were here."

Mr. Howard looked from Santa to Headless and back again. Standing beside Santa, hanging onto his fuzzy red coat, Mr. Howard's jaw moved up and down before the words finally came out. "Santa, help me!"

Santa put his hand on Mr. Howard's shoulder

and said, "Help you? Why, Howie, you're on my naughty list. You must be a good boy before I can help you."

Santa pushed Mr. Howard away. Walking up to Headless and patting him on the back, he said, "How have you been?" He bent down slightly to look into the eyes of Headless. "I'm glad you stopped by tonight."

Mr. Howard leaned against the wall. Nodding his head, he snarled, "I get it. You're all in this together. You got a bunch of actors together and put on this little act to scare me. You're out to get me for trying to buy this place. This is some kind of trick. There's no such thing as Santa or a Headless guy. It's a magic show!"

Essie stood up. "Why, Mr. Howard, you don't believe in Santa Claus? And Headless Horseman? That means you don't believe your own eyes."

Headless walked toward Mr. Howard, holding his head out as it spoke. "Want to hold my head? I'll prove I'm real."

"I'll hold you, Headless," their mother said, taking her son-in-law's most valued possession. "Here, run your fingers through his hair, Mr. Howard." She held the head out in front of Mr. Howard.

The head smiled at him and said, "Boo!"

With a scream from the edge of sanity, Mr. Howard ran outside. Everyone inside the cottage rushed out onto the porch to watch the rest of the plan unfold. Their mother handed Headless his head and went to the door to look out.

Three angry reindeer stood between Mr. Howard and his car, shaking their antlers at him. Mr. Howard stood hunched over, holding his briefcase tightly against his chest as he tried to creep around the reindeer threats. Elvira and Ed were spread-eagled against the car, held there by the threat of being punctured by the antlers of the two reindeer above them. The other three reindeer flew around in the air over the car, sometimes landing on the roof before taking off again.

"Will they hurt him?" Essie whispered to Sharon.

Santa stood beside Sharon and answered, "No! They're playing games with them." He laughed heartily at their antics.

With the grace of a man skirting danger, Mr. Howard made a wide circle around the three reindeer. Two of them took off and hovered above his head. He had his arms over his head and swatted his briefcase at them like flies.

Reaching into his pocket, he pulled out the car keys and with a chirp, opened the doors of the car. Elvira and Ed slid along the car toward the doors. When Mr. Howard reached his car, he flung the door open and a tidal wave of brightly colored eggs came pouring out. The echoes of laughing children filled the air as he kicked them away from around his feet and tried to sweep them out of the car.

Elvira opened the back door and was met with the same multi-colored avalanche. Diving inside, she swam upstream until she was in. Ed followed her into the brightly colored interior.

The reindeer continued to land and kick off from the roof of his car.

Finally, Mr. Howard got into his car with the remaining eggs and started it. The wheels spun gravel back toward the cottage as he hurried to leave. As he left, the reindeer continued to hover above the car like a swarm of gnats.

Essie laughed along with the rest of the group. Easter had his arm around her as they watched their children emerge from the bushes around the cottage. Their mother was standing inside the house, holding her sides as she laughed.

"That was fun!" Thomas yelled out, echoed by Sylvie, Sarah, Clara, and Stacy. All of Essie's children danced around the adults, laughing like they wanted more opportunities to have fun.

"Did you see his face? He was *scared!*" Jason said. Stacy and Sylvie shouted out "yeah!" before the rest of them joined in. Bouncing and running to the porch, they gathered around the adults there, laughing and celebrating the success of their plan.

Essie's mother stood in the house, watching the crowd and laughing at the children's antics.

In the hours that followed Mr. Howard's departure, the families gathered in the living room to enjoy the cake and cookies baked by Sharon earlier. The grandfather clock read nine-fifteen.

Their mother sat in the overstuffed chair. Everyone was gathered around her so they could enjoy her company. The floor was filled with children and the sofa and dining room chairs were filled with the adults. Laughter and chatting filled the room until it almost couldn't hold any more.

Essie noticed her children were no longer afraid of their grandmother, Headless, or his ghostly pirate friends. She hoped they'd learned to accept people as they were. She'd learned the lesson the hard way. They might not be as hard on their siblings, and she wouldn't have to devise a plan to reunite her family, like her mother did.

Her mother must have read her thoughts because she came and sat beside Essie on the sofa. "Your face is sad. Tell me why."

Essie bit her lip. Coming here, she'd been upset at being manipulated. She'd resented it and her mother for doing it. Now she couldn't find a way to say thank you for restoring her relationship with her sisters.

Her mother pulled Essie's head down to her shoulder and stroked her hair, a gesture undone for years. "I know you don't like being forced to do things you don't want to do. Could you be feeling a little guilty because your ol' mom made you play nice with your sisters?" Her mother gave a little chuckle.

Essie returned her chuckle and nodded. "You knew what was best, didn't you. I was a fool for holding a grudge against my sisters and you. My silliness made me miss out on time with you. I regret that more than anything. I'm sorry, Mom." She leaned her head against her mother's cool shoulder and fought back tears.

Her mother patted her cheek and said, "Now now, dear. No one likes being manipulated for someone else's purpose. It's okay to be wary about it, but sometimes you should look at the outcome. Where is someone trying to take you? It could be a better place."

Essie sat up and took a deep breath. "You're wise, and I feel inadequate. I have thirteen children that need guidance. How am I going to do it?"

Her mother waved her arm around the room. "Why, you already have. Look at them! They are playing with their cousins and aunts and uncles. You've given them a sense of the family they belong to, weird as it may be. But they see we can work together to accomplish great things. The cottage is safe for you and for them. I'd say that's pretty good guidance."

"But, Mom—"

Her mother frowned. "Essie, quit overanalyzing! Take things for how they are. This is a happy ending. Enjoy it!"

Essie stared at her mother. Rubbing the tension out of her face, she replied, "You're right as usual, Mother."

Her mother laughed and hugged her daughter. "Of course I am! Now, I need to spend time with Sharon since this is her time with me." She gave a final reassuring pat to Essie before moving to closer to Sharon and Santa.

Before Essie had time to mull over what her mother had told her, Pete and Jason came over.

Pete did the talking, but Jason was barely able to contain himself. "Mom, can we go ride the reindeer? Uncle Santa said we could."

Essie got up off the sofa. "Ride them where?" She looked over at Santa who was smiling at her from the doorway.

Jason was jumping up and down. "Over the ocean. Uncle Santa says that way no one will see us." All her children joined in the begging and pleading.

"He said it was safe, Mom." Jason's hands were woven together as if he were saying an earnest prayer and his eyes were begging her to permit it. How could she say no to those eyes?

Taking Pete by his shoulders, she said, "Let's go

talk to Uncle Santa about it."

Her children gathered around her as she stood in front of Santa. "You're promising my children rides on the reindeer out over the ocean?"

"Ho ho ho! No worries, Essie, the reindeer have harnesses on and they fly smooth as silk. It's like riding a carousel. Sam will ride along, taking the youngest ones with him and making sure no one falls off. They'll have a great time, and the reindeer will get exercise."

A chorus began. "Please, Mom? Please! Please! Please!

Huntley, standing behind the begging children, said, "Mom said me and Horace could go."

The chorus changed its tune to "They get to go. Why can't we? Pleeeeaaassseee!"

What else could she do? "Okay, kids, but if anyone falls off and gets hurt, don't come crying to me!"

With a shout of victory, the throng of cousins ran outside, followed closely by Sam, Santa, Headless, and Easter. The room instantly became quiet, reminding the sisters they had only had a short time to visit with their mother.

The sisters took places on the sofa while their mother sat back in the overstuffed chair. Her eyes closed, but the smile never left her face.

Essie leaned on the arm of the sofa. "Mother, when we were watching the videos, they seemed to know what we were thinking. How did you do that?"

"And who took those videos?" Sharon asked. The three sisters waited for an answer, but all they got was a mysterious smile in return.

"That clock is a wondrous thing," she said. "This

cottage is a magical place. Your father is a wondrous and magical man. That's all I will say about it. There are more important things to discuss about the clock. Come close while I tell you about it. I've been watching over you."

The sisters gathered around their mother as she shared the secrets of the clock. By setting the clock to eight-thirty, she'd watched them in the reflection of the glass of its face. She'd seen their children born and growing. She'd seen their happy lives. She'd been there with them, even though they didn't know it.

Chapter 27

Sharon

Sharon yawned as she stirred the skillet of scrambled eggs. Her sisters weren't up yet, but she'd make something for them when they did rise.

The tent rental people were coming today to take down the tents they'd used last night. She'd make sure the process went smoothly and let her sisters sleep.

Taking a plate out of the cabinet, she placed her buttered toast on it and spooned the eggs beside the toast. She sat alone at the eating bar while she ate, but she didn't mind. Her mind was full of memories of the past few days.

She'd had a talk with her mother and emptied her heart of its guilt. Her mother had forgiven her for everything. Without the weight of the guilt, she felt lighter and happier. A smile covered her face.

As she ate, the children's laughter as they rode the reindeer still rang through her ears. The sweetest sound she'd heard in a long time. Her nieces and nephews had stolen her heart with their hugs, laughter, and gushing over her cookies. They would get extra-special gifts from her this Christmas. Now that she knew them and they knew her, she'd do all she could to grow those relationships in the future.

The chiming doorbell brought her out of her reminiscing. The rental people must already be here to get the tents.

Slinging open the door, she was startled to see two police officers standing there. Sharon wiped her mouth with a napkin still clutched in her hand. "Good morning, officers."

"Hello, ma'am. We're looking for a—" he checked his little notebook. "—Essie Bunny, Sharon Claus, and Hannah Horseman. Do they reside here?"

Sharon noticed his female partner fighting a smile. She smiled, giving the young lady permission to join her. "We have funny names, don't we? Yes, we're here. I'm Sharon Claus by the way. Won't you come in?"

As the officers made their way inside, Essie came out of her bedroom pulling her robe around her. She stopped, startled at the guests. Running her fingers through her hair to straighten it, she came into the living room. "Is there a problem?"

Sharon smiled sweetly at the officers. "Essie, we have company. Anyone want coffee? I brewed a pot. Essie, you look like you could use a cup."

The officers shook their heads, but Essie took her up on the offer. "Do I need to awaken Hannah?"

The female officer shook her head. "I'm Jessica Hanover of the Sarasota County Sheriff Department and this is my training partner, Glen Stanus. We received a report from a Mr. Howard Howard—" the lady fought a smile off again, "—that he was attacked by a headless man, Santa Claus, ghosts, and reindeer last night. He also mentioned something about being sabotaged by a dead woman and the Easter Bunny. It didn't make much sense, although he had a bunch of Easter eggs in his car. Do you have any idea what he was talking about?"

Essie traded a meaningful look with Sharon over the top of her coffee cup. "That sounds pretty wild. He said that happened here?"

Officer Stanus nodded. "He gave us a detailed account of being accosted here last night."

Sharon felt her heart quicken its beating. She held her breath for a moment to stave off hyperventilating. "Was he beat up? I mean 'accosted' is a serious word."

Officer Stanus shook his head. "He had no injuries. We have only his story. He said he had two witnesses, but they refused to talk to us. They kept saying no one would believe it and to leave them alone."

Sharon smoothed her apron. "Sir, only my sisters and I are here. Last night, we had a party for relatives. We were in the tents on the beach enjoying the night. Mr. Howard's not family so he wasn't invited. As far as a headless man and Santa and those other things, it sounds pretty far-fetched to me."

Essie put down her coffee cup. "Had he been drinking?"

Officer Hanover checked her little notebook again. "Not before he saw us, but I'm pretty sure he went to a bar after the alleged incident. He said he was so traumatized he needed a drink. From the way he acted, he had more than one."

"Poor man. Sounds like a really bad dream to

me," Sharon said as she stared at her hands in her lap. She'd never been a good liar. She didn't dare look at the officers lest her eyes give her away.

Essie jumped in. "As you can see, there's been no drunken brawl here. You're free to go look in the tents. You'll find the same there. We had a family gathering last night. We rarely get all of us together. It was a special night for us."

"If Mr. Howard was here, we didn't know it," Sharon said matter-of-factly. "Besides, he'd have been trespassing."

"What's going on here?" Hannah came out of her bedroom, her hair in a mess, and her black nightgown being covered by a black robe. "Why are the police here?"

Sharon filled her in. "They said a man reported being accosted at our house last night. He said a headless man harassed him."

"Really?" She pulled her robe tighter. "Sounds like someone is going crazy to me. Headless people are only found in fairy tales." She yawned and went to the kitchen, soon returning with a cup of coffee.

Officer Hanover fanned herself with her little notebook while Officer Stanus tapped his fingers together. Sharon didn't know if they were waiting to find a hole in their story or if they believed it. Her heart started beating faster, and she felt her breaths coming quickly. Her head started to swirl.

"Sharon," Essie said, "why don't you get these nice officers coffee and that delicious coffee cake you made. And while you're at it, bring me and Hannah some too."

Essie's firm warning look reached Sharon who

jumped to her feet. "Yes, of course." She hurried off to the kitchen where she leaned against the refrigerator for a moment and held her breath. The swirling feeling left. She felt better.

After filling a coffee urn and getting plates and coffee cake, she put a smile on her face before entering the living room again.

"Here we are!" she said in as cheerful a voice as she could muster. "A good way to start the day!" She handed the officers their coffee before slicing the coffee cake for everyone.

The officers took it with words indicating they didn't come to eat, but they ate it anyway.

The sugar-induced smiles on their faces made Sharon relax more. No one could resist her treats.

The conversation turned to pleasantries such as the weather, how nice it was to live next to the beach, and other topics far away from Mr. Howard's supposedly imaginary experiences.

By the end of the visit, Sharon felt relaxed and certain their mother's plan had been executed without any fear of legal fallout.

As the officers stood at the door, Officer Stanus said, "Just my opinion, but I think Howard is having a nervous breakdown. He probably needs rest and counseling. I'll recommend it in my report. Good day, ladies, and thanks for the coffee and treats."

When the officers left, the tent rental people came to take down the tents. The ladies waved from the door of the cottage and went back inside.

Sharon cleared the dishes from the coffee table while her sisters dressed for the day. As she cleaned the kitchen, Essie came in for another cup of coffee. "I thought you might lose it there for a minute."

A nervous laugh escaped Sharon before she knew it. "I'm thankful you sent me to the kitchen. When they sat there not saying anything, I thought they weren't buying our story. My heart took off, and my mind went with it."

"You had an I'm-guilty look on your face. I had to get you out of there." Essie took a sip of coffee and stopped Sharon from putting away the last piece of coffee cake.

Sharon got another piece out of the storage container and joined her.

Hannah came in, dressed in her usual black but wearing a pair of red sequined sneakers. Sharon and Essie stopped in mid-chew to stare. Hannah modeled her new accessory with flourish in front of her stunned sisters.

"What do you think?" She let out a girlish snicker as she sat down with them. "It's my souvenir from this trip."

Finally swallowing the held-back bite, Sharon asked, "When did you get them?"

"When neither of you were looking. I thought I'd do something daring and got them. I think they're kinda fun to wear. And they're comfortable."

"I'm proud of you, sis!" Essie said like a true fan. "You've stepped beyond who you were when you got here which is more than I've done. I bought souvenirs for my kids, but nothing for me."

Sharon let out an excited cry. "I know what we can do. Santa won't be here with the sleigh until way after dark. We have time to go shopping. We'll take a little bit from Mom's stash and spend it on ourselves. I want another blue dress. Or maybe I'll buy a black one!"

A shopping-mania smile spread across Hannah's face and soon spread to Essie's. Sharon felt her face joining in. The sisters were going shopping again!

Chapter 28

Hannah

The sun made its last ray of the day as it dipped below the horizon. Hannah stood on the edge of the water, the waves occasionally reaching her bare toes in the sand. The first stars popped out in the sky behind her. She closed her eyes to feel the breeze and listen to the roar of the ocean as it reached for land. For a few minutes, she was encircled by the halo of twilight.

Taking a deep breath, she turned and went back to the cottage where her sisters were busy getting the place ready to close for a while. Headless had arranged for his pirate ghost friends to stay at the cottage and run off any intruders who might come poking around. He'd given them a method for getting in touch with him if trouble came prowling. The ghoulish security system already patrolled the grounds around the cottage.

Their luggage was in the living room by the front door. After they got home from their shopping trip, Sharon, in her fit of keeping things clean and neat, washed the sheets and towels and everything touched by anyone during their stay.

Hannah and Essie had swept and mopped while Sharon scrubbed. Together they made short work of the housecleaning chores. The place was pristine like their mother kept it.

As Hannah approached the cottage, she saw her sisters on the front porch deep in conversation. The sight made her heart light and her face smile. A week ago, they hated each other. Hated each other so much they'd no contact with each other for years. Through their mother's brilliant manipulation, they were friends.

Climbing the steps, Essie motioned for Hannah to take the other seat on the porch swing. Her red sequined shoes were there, waiting for her to put them on. They matched her black leggings and red and black tunic. Glamorous. That's how she felt, and she loved it.

Essie sat on the other end of the porch swing in her flowered jacket over a textured black tank top with her black slacks. A red and gold necklace matched her jacket. Like her sister, she'd bought a pair of sequined shoes, light green to match her outfit.

Hannah had helped her with a little bit of makeup. She thought her sister looked years younger with it on. A little makeup and a new outfit made her look like a million bucks.

Sharon leaned back in a wicker chair with her feet propped up on a small table. Her black dress with the blue flowers spread across the fabric was pulled up to her pudgy white knees as she gazed out toward the ocean.

Hannah thought she looked younger too. The cottage had had a revitalizing effect on all of them.

Hannah closed her eyes, letting Essie swing her

back and forth. She didn't want the moment to end. It was too peaceful to end. Too special to end. But soon Santa and his sleigh would come to pick them up. No airline flight this time. This time, first-class service by Santa and the elves.

Hannah broke the blissful silence, saying, "When I have my turn calling Mom back for my visit with her, I'd like for the two of you to be here."

Essie stopped rocking the porch swing. "Really?"

"Why, Hannah!" Sharon said. "That's one of the nicest things I've ever heard!"

Hannah looked at her sisters. "It makes sense. You took your one turn, Sharon, when we were here. You let our children get to know her. Why do it once? If we are together when we each take our turn, we get to see Mom two more times. Not just once."

Sniffing took over where silence had once been. Sharon, digging through her purse, found a tissue and wiped her nose. "That's the nicest gift anyone could ever give. Time with Mom." She wiped her nose again and dried her eyes. "Thanks, Hannah."

"That's a great idea," Essie said, her voice wobbly with emotion. "I'll do the same and share my time with Mom with you too. I'd like for our families to be here, if Santa doesn't mind flying me and my brood over."

Sharon wiped her nose again. "I don't think Uncle Santa minds at all."

Hannah pushed the swing with her toe. "I love that we have more time with her. She seemed happy to see us together. I'd like to see her happy again."

Essie and Sharon muttered their agreement.

"My boys enjoyed seeing their cousins. Huntley has already asked when they get to see them again. They enjoyed playing with them."

Sharon sat up. "I hope Sam can come again. I'm not sure if his college schedule would allow it, but maybe so."

Hannah nodded. "I look forward to the next time we're together."

Silence returned to the porch as the sisters went their own way with their thoughts.

Shutting her eyes, Hannah focusing on the sounds and smell of the cottage, the beach, and the ocean. Her heart smiled. What a beautiful place! And it was theirs to visit whenever they wanted.

She wondered if her sisters felt the same way. "Any regrets?' she said aloud.

Silence floated in the air until Sharon spoke. "None."

Essie took in a deep breath of the fresh air. "I regret it took Mom's scheming and manipulation to get us back to being sisters. Otherwise I have no regrets. I'm glad we own this little piece of heaven. I love that we can call our father whenever we need him. I love I can bring my children here and someday, after I'm gone, I can come back to see them once more."

Hannah laughed. "Once more? You'll be back thirteen times! You'll have to schedule appointments."

Sharon didn't laugh along. "I'll only come back once."

"Most people never come back at all," Hannah said softly. "Let's be thankful for the privilege, no matter how often it is."

"True," Sharon said in a whisper barely heard

above the rustling of the beach grass.

While one more day alone with her mother would have been one of her life's greatest privilege, she had no regrets about sharing her day. The cottage was safe. Her sons met their grandmother. She'd spent four hours alone with her mother. That time had been as precious as anything she'd ever known.

The sky grew darker until only the stars lit the sky. Sharon snored softly. Essie's head bobbed a time or two as she drifted off.

The breeze dried Hannah's tears and cooled her face. She fought to stay awake. The chore was made easier when a silent figure came onto the porch.

"Right on time, Rummy Jones," Hannah whispered to the floating figure. "Where's Peg Leg?"

"He be not far behind me," he said as he came closer. "We'll keep a close watch on ya place 'ere. We let ya know ifn som'thin' be happenin'."

Hannah nodded. "I expect it will be well taken care of. Enjoy the house, but don't mess it up! We want it in good shape when we come back to visit."

"Don' ya worry ya little head none," Peg Leg said as he came from behind Hannah. He drifted past her and joined Rummy Jones. "It's a right nice place to hang out. We'll take good care of it."

"Good." Hannah yawned and stretched as their security team floated into the wall and inside the house. The sound of soft bells reached her ears and she knew it was time.

Shaking Essie from her slumber, she got out of the porch swing and roused Sharon. "I think Santa's almost here."

Even in her half-wakefulness, Sharon smiled as

she heard the soft bells too. "Vacation's over, girls!" She went into the house to get her luggage.

Hannah heard Sharon yell before she came running back outside, wild-eyed and shaking. Essie held her until her fright quieted.

Rummy Jones appeared through the wall. "Sorry abou' tha' mate. Didn't mean to scare ya!"

Hannah continued rocking in the porch swing as she said, "I forgot to tell you our guards were here. I should have warned you. At least we know our system works."

Sharon sat in the wicker chair again. "Scared me out of ten years of life. The cottage should be safe with them around."

With a soft thud, a red sleigh landed in front of the cottage. The stomping of tiny feet and a squeaking leather harness was heard before Santa tromped up the porch steps. Sharon was in his arms in one leap.

"Ho ho ho! What's this welcome? Does that mean you're ready to go home?"

"Yes, indeed! I've missed you and the elves."

Hannah went inside and brought their luggage out to the porch.

Two elves grabbed it and hauled it to the sleigh. Even with their short stature and light weight, they were strong and agile. They handled their luggage easily before getting back on the sleigh again, waving for the others to get on board.

Santa helped Sharon into the front seat beside his own. He held his hand toward the other two sisters. Essie bolted from the porch and with a single bound, jumped aboard the tall sleigh. Sitting behind Santa, she nestled herself into the seat.

Hannah laughed silently as she locked the door and waved a farewell to the two ghosts standing near the door of the cottage as she went down the steps. She stepped into the sleigh and sat beside Essie on the red leather seat.

The two elves who sat on top of their luggage behind them gave them each a woolen blanket in case they needed it as they traveled north.

The rush of being lifted off the ground by reindeer made Hannah's stomach flutter with butterflies. She gave one quick glance back at the cottage on the beach, lit only by starlight. She looked forward to coming here again.

Hannah smiled as the sleigh turned and headed north. She'd be home before Halloween.

About the Author

The author spent her life doing many different things. She's been a teacher, a statistician, a literacy tutor, an archeological technician, and best of all, a technical writer/editor. Now retired, she loves to quilt, sew, and write in her home in the Pacific Northwest where she lives with her husband.

She has self-published several novels, one children's book, and a non-fiction book are available from Kindle and Amazon.

The author's last name is pronounced "care." She hopes that's what everyone will do. Care about each other.

Other Books by C.S. Kjar:

The Treasure of Adonis

Blessings From the Wrong Side of Town

The Five Grannies Go to the Ball

Scraps of Wisdom: All I Needed to Know I
Learned in Quilting Class

For more information:

Visit my website at http://cskjar.com

and my Facebook page at
http://www.facebook.com/cskjar

Contact me at cskjar.books@gmail.com

You can also follow me on Twitter at @cskjar

Asking a big favor...

If you enjoyed this novel, please write a review for it at one or more of your favorite retailers or readers sites. Even a short review, one or two lines, can be a tremendous help to me. Your review is also a gift to other readers who may be searching for a story like this and will be grateful you helped them find it.

If you write a review, please send me an email at cskjar.books@gmail.com so I can thank you with a personal reply. Also, let me know when you tell your friends, readers' groups, and discussion boards about this book.

Thank you very much for your support. C.S. Kjar

ACKNOWLEDGEMENTS

First and foremost, thanks to my husband who has put up with me all these decades and supports me in my writing career. Thanks to my children who have always encouraged me to follow my dreams.

Thanks also to all those who helped me with this book. My beta readers and support groups give me great advice and constructive criticism.

The Daughters of Time:

Book Two

The Secrets of the Cottage

Essie Bunny, Sharon Claus, and Hannah Horseman return to Florida when neighbors complain of flashing lights and strange noises coming from the cottage. They find unexpected guests who refuse to leave.

Negotiating a deal, the unwanted visitors will leave when the sisters find a missing person. With their unwelcome visitors in the cottage, they dare not use the clock to call their father or mother for help. The sisters are perplexed.

How do they find a person who has been missing for many years? How will they persuade the intruders to leave without meeting the terms of their agreement?

Made in the USA
Monee, IL
07 May 2023

32960935R00148